ME AND
MY BOI

ME AND MY BOI

GAY EROTIC STORIES

EDITED BY
SACCHI GREEN

CLEiS
PRESS

Published in the United States by Cleis Press, an imprint of Start Midnight, LLC, 101 Hudson Street, 37th Floor, Suite 3705, Jersey City, NJ 07302.

Printed in the United States.
Cover design: Scott Idleman/Blink
Cover Photo: ThinkStock
Text design: Frank Wiedemann
First Edition.
10 9 8 7 6 5 4 3 2 1

Trade paper ISBN: 978-1-62778-121-3
E-book ISBN: 978-1-62778-139-8

Contents

INTRODUCTION

This book is a celebration of all things boi, butch and masculine-of-center, in those who include lesbian as a part of their identities. These are stories of people we love, and people we are, who put their own personal spins on the gender spectrum. Bois who like girls, bois who like bois, bois who like both; those who don't label themselves boi or butch at all but can't stand to wear a skirt; screw-the-binary free spirits of many flavors. Cool bois, hot bois, swaggering bois, shy bois, leather bois, flannel bois, butch daddies and the femmes and mommas and tops and bottoms and even girls next door who wouldn't have them any other way.

Writers always blow me away with the variety in their stories, and the twenty here are no exception. Some are from a boi's point of view, some from a femme's, some from a seasoned butch's. Some deal with youthful self-discovery and others with finding your inner butch later in life. The settings range from a charming English garden and an equally charming (if greasy) English car-repair garage, to a racing sailboat, to quiet forests and rushing cities and dimly lit bedrooms where the rest of the world might as well not exist. A couple of pieces take us back through time, to a Regency drawing room and an old-school, pre-Stonewall lesbian blue-collar bar, but most could be taking place just yesterday, or today, or tomorrow.

And, of course, all these stories give us a charge of steamy, explicit sex that develops naturally out of all the elements in the story. The action may be kinky, or hard-edged, or sweet, or passionately emotional—or even blends of those that you wouldn't have thought possible—but whatever turns you on, or cuts deep, or sparks your wildest fantasies, if these writers don't push the buttons you already have, maybe they'll hook you up with some new ones. Gender has no boundaries, and neither does lust.

Sacchi Green
Amherst, MA

ONLY PINUP

Gigi Frost

She is my only pinup. Half-asleep in the morning, I roll over to watch her dress, enjoying every stage, boxer briefs tight around her thighs, bra or binder showing her strong shoulders, over that a white undershirt, the way she walks around with her jeans undone while she puts on deodorant and buttons her shirt.

She is my only pinup, sprawled on my bed, hands behind her head, grinning up at me. She is the strongest, the softest, the only one I want. I love kissing her powerful back, her sharp curving hip bones. I can't stop grabbing her butt whenever I am behind her, in the kitchen when she's washing dishes, or just walking down the hall.

There are girls like me everywhere, pretty office workers pouring out onto downtown streets in pencil skirts and heels, interns with long shiny hair at the State House, models half-naked on billboards, every blockbuster movie populated by virgins and whores. If she wants a little eye candy, all she has to do is open her eyes.

My type is butch, or transmasculine, et cetera. And they do

catch my eye sometimes, salt-and-pepper butches at the co-op bundled in flannel and fleece, sporty dykes in Provincetown, walking the streets in cargo shorts and polo shirts, their hair sticky with wax. But you won't find my type baring their skin to sell Skittles or shaving cream. If I want to look at a handsome pair of arms, or the hidden curve of a strong chest, well, I'm lucky I have my very own pinup right here in my bedroom, getting dressed.

She is my only pinup. I joke about making a calendar, six months of her in a binder and boxer briefs in different colors, three months in a sports bra and jeans, three months in a shirt and tie, maybe a sweater vest for variety.

When we watch movies, she watches the men, their clothes, their hair, their bodies. Walking down the street, she'll grab my arm. "He's so tall!" "Did you see his jacket?" I turn my head, but the object of this admiration, envy or wonder is halfway down the block. "I didn't notice," I mumble. If anything, I notice women, their colors, their accessories, their posture.

In the country of men, she is a foreign exchange student with a visa and I don't even have a passport. She is writing a doctoral thesis and I don't speak the language. I never needed to, never wanted to. I am an admirer of this masculinity, I don't need to embody it.

She is my only pinup, my butch and my top. Her desire to fuck me is an electrical current that charges and changes us both. I don't need to fuck her in the same way. I don't have that energy coursing through me that makes we want to take her, own her.

When I fuck her it's sweet, silly, gentle, so different from how she tops me, with that scary look that melts me, makes me arch my back and throw my hands up over my head.

The first time she let me touch her chest, it was morning. She asked me to look away while she took off her binder, then crawled under the sheet, pulled it up to her chin like a child afraid of monsters who will snatch anything left uncovered. She let me touch her back. The sheets, the walls, her skin, all pale, reflected the sunlight that poured in and we were late for work again, like we always were that summer.

I kissed her neck, the freckles behind her ears, and she said, coy like a femme, "I have freckles on my back, too." I kissed the bone ridges of her spine, the sheet still pulled up to her waist. We rolled over together, skin to skin like some mad ballet, and there is nothing, nothing, like chests and nipples touching. Especially when I had wondered if it would ever happen.

We'd talked about someday, talked about how she dreamed of lying topless on the beach, but I thought it would be months, years, before she'd let me touch her chest. I would stroke her belly while we cuddled and sometimes she asked me to massage under the elastic band of her sports bra where her skin was sore and constricted. Gradually, we were getting closer to something we both knew we wanted. Later, I joked it only took me six months to get to second base.

After that day she gradually got more comfortable. Soon she had a new pinup pose, on her back, chest bare with her hands behind her head, grinning up at me.

And then, just a few weeks later, we woke up on another morning, kissing and touching, and she asked me to fuck her.

Warm skin against skin, my mouth everywhere, on her cunt, my hands cupping her hip bones, grasping her breasts. I kissed from the hollow of her breast up to her chin and back down again. She pushed the pillows up over her head, arched her back and let me in.

Right before I enter her there's always a little hesitation, looking both ways, peering around the corner. But then—the long slow entrance, and she is so ready for me, keeps opening and I add another finger, and another. She keeps arching up, trying to get close enough to kiss me, but I want to go deeper, so I push her back down.

I love seeing the silhouette of her buzzed head against the pillow. Fucking her like this I get a taste of the power she wields over me, but I get self-conscious, I need her to tell me what feels right, I need us both to laugh when I all but do a back bend to reach the lube, which has of course rolled under the bed.

I love how wet she gets, just from making out, just from thinking about fucking me, about hurting me. I lean over her, kissing, grinding, and she tells me that she wants everything, wants to flip me over and fuck me at the same time that she also wants to get fucked. If she can't decide, I'll decide for her.

"Don't go getting all fierce just yet," I say, and push her over onto her back.

This is love, and passion, and trust, and I get to look all I want while she comes on my hand.

A FRESH START

Melissa Mayhew

B ob lay on her back on the creeper, looking up at the under-side of a car that, in her view, should have been consigned to the great scrapyard in the sky long ago. Grimly, she applied the socket and bar and exerted all her muscle power to the bottom ball joint. If it didn't budge soon, she was going to burn the damn thing off. Grunting, she forced her weight against it. It didn't budge.

"Come on, you bastard," she muttered under her breath, levering the bar hard. She felt the sweat running down her face, the strain in her muscles and then, finally, she felt a tiny move-ment as years of muck and rust gave way and it began to turn.

She relaxed, catching a breath. This bloody wreck was going to be the death of her. But the owner loved it, and despite the expense, insisted on the garage keeping it on the road, no matter what.

"Bob, kettle's on," she heard Ed shout across the noise of the workshop.

"Okay, coming," she called.

"Lucky cow."

She heard a burst of male laughter, and grinned. As the only girl in the workshop, she was often the butt of male colleagues' jokes, but she gave as good as she got, and they were all close friends who'd known each other for years.

Not that it was true, she thought, her smile fading. It had been a bloody long time since she'd got lucky. Not since Lauren had left, five years before, in fact. Since then, she hadn't much bothered with romance, but now and again she missed it.

Sighing, she emerged from the underside of the car, wiping the sweat from her forehead, and went to get her tea.

The bell on the customer counter rang just as she picked up her mug. Damn. As a small garage, they didn't have a receptionist, and anyone who was available went to serve when customers came in.

Wiping her hands on her boiler suit, she walked through to the customer area and saw a look of surprised relief wash across the pretty elfin features of the small brunette who stood waiting. Bob smiled easily. It wasn't uncommon for female customers to feel intimidated in the largely male environment of the garage, and she often helped to put them at ease.

"Hi. Can I help you?"

The brunette looked sheepishly into her eyes. "I hope so. My car's making a weird noise. I've no idea…" She trailed off.

"Okay. Why don't you have a seat, and we'll take a look at it. Do you have the keys?"

"Oh. Yes." The woman slid a voluminous handbag from her shoulder, and raked through it. Bob laughed. "Looks like you've got the kitchen sink in there."

The woman grimaced. "Just about literally. I'm just moving into the area. Basically, all my worldly goods are in the car, and this bag."

Bob nodded, thinking how very sexy the woman was, with

her smooth, dark hair, soft, curvy figure and small, slender hands.

"You've landed a job near here?"

"Uh-huh. Research assistant at the university. I only got the job last week, but they wanted me to start straightaway, so here I am. I've had to rent a house I've never even seen—some place nearby called Tanfield Village."

Bob started. "Oh! You must have rented the old Mill House."

The woman's eyes widened. "How did you—?"

"ESP?"

The woman blushed. "You wouldn't want to read my mind."

Bob's eyebrows rose. "No?"

She laughed nervously. "I wouldn't want to shock you."

"Sweetheart, that's highly unlikely." The endearment came naturally, unexpectedly, and for a moment, the two women looked at each other, a thousand unspoken thoughts swirling between them.

Bob cleared her throat, striving for normality. "I live in Tanfield. It's a small village, and that's the only place up for rent just now. It's a nice house, you'll like it."

"Oh! We'll be neighbors, then?"

"Mmm-hmm."

"In that case I'll introduce myself. I'm Ellie."

"Bob. Good to meet you."

Bob looked into Ellie's pretty blue eyes and wondered if the color deepened when she was aroused. She could just imagine peeling off that fluffy little sweater, revealing the rounded curves of Ellie's breasts, stroking the vulnerable tenderness of her stomach, hearing sighs and groans as her work-hardened hands slid across smooth skin lower to soft, moist warmth. Would she taste as good as she looked? Bob felt her stomach clench at the thought. Hell, she loved the scent and taste of an aroused woman, to bury her head—

The door banged as another customer walked in. Bob jolted back to the present, shocked. Hell, what was she thinking? She was at work, for goodness sake. Not only that, she never, ever flirted with customers; it was a recipe for disaster.

She frowned as she looked at Ellie's head, lowered now as she rummaged in her handbag. Had Ellie guessed what she was thinking? Had she embarrassed her? She didn't want Ellie to feel awkward around her, especially if they were going to be neighbours.

Ellie looked up, smiling. "Found them," she said, handing the keys over, but her tone was brittle, and Bob noticed that she wouldn't meet her eyes. Shit.

"If you'll take a seat, I'll get your car looked at," Bob said, politely, and watched as Ellie turned and sat down. Forcing a smile to her face, she turned to greet the other customer.

Ellie hadn't been joking about the kitchen sink, Bob discovered ten minutes later as she reversed the little Auris over a bay. The back was so full of stuff that you couldn't see out of the rear window.

As she maneuvred the car she listened to a rhythmic knocking in the engine. A pound to a penny, the suspension arm bush had gone. And if that was the case, Ellie wasn't going anywhere, as they'd have to order the part in overnight and fit it the next day.

Half an hour later, Bob's diagnosis was confirmed. Ellie's face, when Bob told her, was a picture of dismay. "I don't believe this," she muttered. "Could anything else go wrong this week?"

"You'll be on the move again tomorrow," Bob said reassuringly.

"Yes, but I wanted to get settled in tonight. All my stuff's in the back." Her shoulders slumped. "Never mind," she sighed, pulling a mobile phone out of her pocket. "You don't happen to have the number of a local taxi firm, do you?"

Bob hesitated. It was nearly five, and she was due to finish. She could easily give her a lift.

The offer was made before Bob had time to process the wisdom of it. She watched an expression of thanks and relief cross the pretty face. "Really? That would be great."

Half an hour later, Bob's estate car was loaded with Ellie's belongings, and they set off along the pretty country roads toward the village.

"I had no idea it was so lovely around here," Ellie exclaimed as they drove along the country lanes lined with pink dog roses and creamy white cow parsley.

Bob nodded, trying to ignore the subtle allure of Ellie's floral scent. "It's a good location. Close enough to the city for work, but far enough away from the madding crowd."

Ellie looked at her, surprised. "Madding? You like Thomas Hardy?"

"Sure. I prefer his poetry to his prose, though. You?"

"Oh, yes. I love both."

They drew up outside the Mill House. Bob turned to look at her. "You didn't expect a mechanic to read Hardy?"

Ellie's eyes widened. "Well, I..."

Bob grinned. "You'll find I don't conform to much. I just do what suits me. I love mechanics, I love reading, I love..." She broke off, looking away. "Well, I am who I am."

Ellie stared at her. "I am surprised," she admitted. "Not because you're a mechanic, but because very few people read Hardy these days, especially his poetry."

"You have."

"Well, yes. But then—"

"Then what?"

"Well, it's my job. That's what I do. I'm a researcher in English."

* * *

The Mill House delighted Ellie, who exclaimed in delight at the period features, the gorgeous view of the river and the pretty cottage garden. Following a tour of the house, Bob helped her unload the contents of the car into the drawing room.

"Good grief, I'm done in," said Ellie as they hauled in the last box. Sitting on top of it, she stretched, wiped a limp strand of hair from her face and then laughed at the sight of Bob. "You don't look like you've even broken into a sweat!"

Bob shrugged, avoiding Ellie's eyes. With her job, she used her muscles every day and carrying in a few boxes was hardly an effort. But seeing Ellie sitting there like that, sweaty and rumpled, had her on the rack. She wanted to go over there, lay her back over the box, pull off her jeans and—

Bob turned abruptly and headed for the door. "I'll leave you to it. If you like I'll pick you up tomo—"

She stiffened as Ellie jumped off the box and caught hold of her arm. "Bob? Wait. What is it? What's wrong?"

Bob felt her muscles clench at the light touch; she couldn't help it. She jerked away, raking a frustrated hand through her short, dark hair. She could smell Ellie's perfume and the musky scent of her sweat, and her stomach clenched. "Ellie, nothing's wrong. I just have to go."

"Bob, please. Let me at least treat you to something to eat to say thanks for helping me. Didn't I see a pub just along the road?"

Bob shut her eyes. She could tell how much Ellie wanted her to stay. She should take her to the pub, and introduce her to some of the locals, help her to make friends. It was just that it was so damn hard to be around her, feeling so aroused that she was caught on a knife-edge of pleasure and pain. She didn't even know if Ellie was straight, gay, or somewhere in between, and she had no intention of coming on to someone who might be horrified by an approach.

"Ellie…"

"Bob…"

They both paused, then Ellie said diffidently, "Bob, can I talk to you frankly? I know I haven't known you long, but I feel like I have."

Bob turned warily, folding her arms. "What is it?"

Ellie moved to look out of the window, her body tense. "Earlier, I said this week couldn't get much worse."

"Yes."

"My boyfriend split up with me."

Bob felt her stomach plummet. Ellie was straight. End of story. "More fool him," she said, roughly. "He'd have to be crazy to give up a girl like you."

Ellie shook her head. "Not really. I… I…" She turned to face Bob, her eyes anguished. "He left me because…because I'm rubbish in bed."

For a moment, Bob's face went blank as a hundred thoughts vied for attention in her head. Finally, she asked, "Why?"

"Why am I rubbish at it?"

Bob nodded.

Ellie blushed. "I could never fancy him," she said in a low voice. "He was a nice guy but I just didn't…like it. I tried, because I wanted not to be…" She broke off, staring at her feet.

Bob's jaw clenched. "Just tell me," she said.

"I wanted not to be attracted to women."

"But you are?"

"Y-yes. I… I'm attracted to you."

Bob closed her eyes, feeling torn. She knew that it had taken a good deal of courage and trust for Ellie to confide in her. But if she let Ellie get close, she risked getting hurt again, and last time had been bad enough. Her jaw firmed. For five years, she'd lived like a nun. Perhaps it was time to take a risk.

"Come here," she said.

Ellie looked relieved but nervous. Bob could see the tension in her small frame, and rolled her eyes. "You can calm down," she said, dryly. "If you think I'm about to make love to you after a hard day's work dressed in an oily boiler suit, you've got another thing coming."

"Oh." Ellie relaxed visibly.

"How about we go to my place, so I can have a shower and get changed? Then the pub for a meal. After that, we'll see how it goes. There's no need to rush anything. I've waited five years, I can wait a bit longer if need be."

"Five years?"

"It's been a long time. I don't take casual lovers."

Ellie flushed. "I don't think this would be casual," she murmured.

"No. I don't think it would be, either."

"So, where's your place?"

"Ah." Bob paused. "Well, actually, it's next door."

Bob left Ellie browsing the bookshelves in the study and went upstairs to shower and change into her usual black jeans, black shirt and leather jacket, with a low-slung belt circling her narrow hips. The style suited her tall, boyish figure and her casual approach to life.

She picked up her wallet, went downstairs, and found Ellie sitting at the kitchen table browsing through a book of poems. Ellie's eyes widened as she walked in.

"What is it?"

"You look different in normal clothes."

Bob frowned. "Different?"

"Tough. Powerful. Sexy."

"Sounds scary. Want to back out?"

"No!"

"Well then, let's go. Tough, powerful, sexy women need to

keep their energy up, you know."

They enjoyed excellent roast beef and a very good real ale, and sat chatting by the fire afterward. Bob was pleased to see Ellie relax and laugh.

Finally, they walked home. Bob slung a casual arm around Ellie's shoulders. Ellie hesitated, then slowly stretched her own arm around Bob's back, to rest a hand at her waist.

They reached the house. "I know it's a little soon to ask this, but would you like to come in with me?" Bob asked softly, looking into Ellie's wide eyes.

Slowly, Ellie nodded. Taking her trembling hand, Bob led her inside. "I'm going to take you to my bedroom. Okay?" she murmured.

A sharp, jerky nod. The lady looked like she was suffering from an extreme case of nerves. Bob led her upstairs. She was going to have to make Ellie relax somehow, or this was going to be a disaster.

The bedroom, with its cream walls and neutral shades of taupe and chocolate brown, was lit only by the glow of a small bedside lamp. Bob sat on the large, soft bed and patted the counterpane beside her. "Sit down," she invited.

Ellie sat.

"I thought perhaps we could talk first," Bob said mildly.

Ellie's eyes flew to hers. "Okay."

"Have you ever done anything at all with a woman before?"

"No."

"Well, you don't have to do anything now, either, if you don't want to." Bob rested her hand on Ellie's. "If you're not ready, we can wait. Don't beat yourself up about it."

Ellie flushed. "I really want to do this with you. I'm just afraid that..."

"What?"

"I told you. I'm no good in bed. What if I disappoint you?"

Bob grimaced. So that was what all the nerves were about. She should have realized.

"Sweetheart, all I want you to do is relax. Leave everything to me."

Bob stood up. She slung her leather jacket over the edge of the bedroom chair and turned to face the tense figure perched on her bed. "Lie down," she commanded.

Ellie hesitated, and then did as she was told. Bob knelt on the bed and gently pulled off Ellie's shoes. "Do you like having your feet rubbed?"

"Y-yes."

"Good."

Bob began to massage her feet with firm fingers, rubbing the arches and caressing the toes. She kept going until she saw Ellie's slim body relax against the soft pillows, and then let her hands drift slowly upward to massage the soft denim encasing her calves. Ellie's eyes fluttered shut as she absorbed the relaxing sensations, and gradually Bob slid her hands up toward her knees and then onto her thighs. The bedroom was quiet except for their soft breathing, as Bob parted Ellie's legs and slid her hands slowly upward toward her inner thighs. There she paused, massaging the fabric, knowing it would be rubbing and teasing the sensitive regions between Ellie's legs. She heard Ellie's breathing quicken, felt the instinctive undulating movements of her hips and smiled.

Stroking the fabric in slow, teasing circles, she watched as Ellie's movements became more abandoned, her flush deepening. Finally, Ellie opened her eyes.

"Please," she whispered.

"Please what?"

"I'm so close."

Bob reached up and stroked her hair. "Take off your jeans," she said huskily.

Ellie's eyes widened, and then hurriedly she pulled them off.

"Good girl. Now lie back."

Ellie lay back, trembling.

"Open your legs."

Slowly, Ellie let them fall open.

"Wider."

Biting her lip, Ellie complied.

She was wearing pretty little white panties, and Bob could see the damp patch and smell the musky scent of her arousal.

"My, my," she said gently, running a teasing finger over the damp cotton, "aren't we aroused."

"Oh!" Ellie flushed scarlet, and went to close her legs. Quickly, Bob caught her knees. "No, sweetheart. Keep them open for me. Sit up and take off your sweater."

Lightly, Bob tickled across the white cotton. Ellie bucked and squealed, and then struggled out of her sweater to reveal a white lacy bra.

Casually, Bob reached up and pulled down the delicate bra cups, exposing the creamy swell of Ellie's breasts. She watched as the cool night air made the nipples pucker and tighten, and then ran a work-roughened thumb gently over one sensitive tip. Ellie cried out, arching. Her breath came in short panting gasps as Bob moved her hands to stroke lightly around the blushing areolas, her drifting fingers never quite straying to the aching, wanting nipples.

Ellie felt a flood of wet warmth soak her panties and twisted helplessly. But the light pressure of Bob's fingers kept on tormenting and circling until Ellie was bathed in sweat. Only then did Bob stretch out her long, slim body beside her and lower herself to take one soft, rounded breast into her mouth.

Ellie gasped as she felt for the first time the gentle suckle of a warm woman's mouth. Bob's tongue stroked and swirled softly around the nipple, and then, at Ellie's abandoned response, stiffened to rasp firmly against the sensitive flesh.

Ellie, crying out, clutched at Bob's head, pressing it to her breast.

"Please! Oh, Bob, please..."

And then she felt Bob reach down into her wet panties, stroking strong, powerful fingers between her pussy lips, to slide smoothly inside her.

The feeling of Bob's powerful hand massaging her inside, whilst her demanding mouth suckled on her breast, sent Ellie spiraling. She was dimly aware of Bob raising herself onto her elbow, and then the hand in her panties moved so that even as the fingers worked their magic the heel of the hand pressed hard against her clitoris.

Sensation blossomed as Ellie squirmed, crying out, stretching her legs wide open to bear down on Bob's hand. Her breasts ached, her pussy throbbed. She sobbed in torment as the powerful surge of impending orgasm roiled, and then suddenly Bob reared up, holding her down with one powerful hand whilst the other massaged her inside and out with a fierce pressure in quick, circular movements that sent Ellie screaming in drenched abandon straight over the edge.

Afterward, Bob pulled an exhausted, trembling Ellie into her arms.

"I never knew..."

"Shh. It's okay. Go to sleep."

"But what about you?"

"It doesn't matter. Get some rest, honey."

Bob watched as Ellie slid helplessly into sleep in her arms, and smiled tenderly, stroking the hair back from her face. It had been good for her, and Bob felt an overwhelming sense of satisfaction that the first, crucial time had gone well. Ellie was an amazing woman. Bob's gut tightened at the memory of her passion and she shifted restlessly, her own body aching with need.

But whilst Ellie had enjoyed being touched by a woman, she had not yet confronted the reality of touching another woman's body. It was possible she wouldn't like it. Especially with her, Bob thought, bleakly.

She remembered Lauren's wounding words as she'd left with a petite, pneumatic blonde on her arm. "Look at you. You're more a man than a woman," she'd sneered. "I want a womanly woman."

Well, if there was one thing she would never be, it was a womanly woman. Her body was tall, slim, muscular, closer to the ideal body shape for a man. Her instinctive outlook and approach to life could broadly be described as masculine. She couldn't change that. Would Ellie, like Lauren, leave her for a softer, curvier, more feminine lover? The thought of another rejection sliced into her, and she winced inwardly.

Sighing, she pulled a comforter over them both. She'd just have to hope for the best. Dropping a tired kiss on Ellie's hair, she closed her eyes, breathed in the warm, musky scent of the pretty, feminine body next to her, and went to sleep.

Two hours later, she awoke abruptly, flinching at the unexpected sensation of someone touching her.

"Bob! Bob, it's me. Ellie."

"Oh!" Bob subsided back against the pillow with a sigh. Sleep-dazed, she mumbled without thinking, "Sorry. I'm not used to being touched."

There was a moment's silence. Then Ellie said warily, "I'm sorry. I shouldn't have…"

"I said I wasn't used to it, not that I minded." Stretching out her arm, she pulled in Ellie by her side and kissed her hair, drowsily. Ellie laid her head on Bob's shoulder.

"Bob?" she whispered.

"Mmm?"

"What you did earlier was amazing. But…"

"But…?"

"But I want to touch you, too."

Sleep fled in an instant, the tension in Bob's body unmistakable.

Ellie sat up, and looked into her lover's evasive eyes. "What's the matter?"

"Nothing."

"Don't lie to me. What's wrong?"

For a moment there was silence. Then Bob said, flatly, "You've never touched a woman. You might not like it. And my body"—she paused, then went on with difficulty—"it's not like yours. Yours is curvy, soft, delicious. Mine is harder, more muscular. Not…so attractive."

Ellie looked at her, aghast. "You're worried I don't find your body attractive?" Bob's eyes slid away from hers. "Or perhaps," Ellie said quietly, "you don't think anybody would find it attractive."

Bob winced, and Ellie's eyes narrowed. "Five years since you last had a lover. Is that how long you've believed that?"

The silence stretched.

Ellie swallowed hard on a surge of protective fury. Some bitch had really done a number on Bob, but she was damned if she was going to let her continue to think of herself as unattractive. Rubbish lover or not, she was going to show Bob exactly how attractive she found her.

"Well, there's only one way to show you how I feel, isn't there?" said Ellie, finally. "Will you let me touch you?"

Bob swallowed. There was nothing she wanted more than to have Ellie touch her, but the memory of Lauren's harsh words was ringing in her ears. Finally, she forced herself to reply. For better or worse, she needed to know if Ellie could accept her body.

"I…yes."

Ellie expelled a harsh breath. "Thank you," she breathed.

Bob felt Ellie's hand go to her shirt, and flinched involuntarily. Ellie froze, and then leaned over to look into her wary eyes. "Bob, would you mind if we kissed first?'" she asked.

"No."

Slowly, Ellie lowered her head and pressed what she hoped was a reassuring kiss onto Bob's lips. She felt them part beneath her own, and then the heat rose in her and she thrust her arm under Bob's neck and lifted up her head to kiss her with all the pent-up power and passion this woman kindled in her. Beneath her mouth, she heard Bob gasp, and then she thrust her tongue inside and kissed her with a ferocity and intensity born partly of an overwhelming fury that someone could have hurt Bob, and partly out of a desperate need to show how desirable she found her.

As she kissed her, Ellie used her free hand to undo the buttons of Bob's shirt, and then slid it inside to caress her small, firm breasts. Under her mouth, Bob groaned as she rolled the taut little nipples between her thumb and forefinger, and Ellie felt her shudder under the rough caress.

Ellie bent her head to draw the firm flesh into her mouth, licking and sucking the beautiful globes with exhilarating abandon. She had always, always wanted to touch a woman's breasts, but touching Bob's made her feel indescribably tender and powerful. Beneath her ministrations, Bob sobbed and writhed helplessly.

Without missing a beat, Ellie yanked off Bob's belt, unbuttoned her jeans, and thrust them down over her narrow hips. Bob's panties were black and high cut, accentuating the magnificent length of her beautiful legs. Ellie felt a surge of desire, and immediately thrust her hand downward.

Bob cried out and arched, gasping, as Ellie slammed two fingers hard inside her, and then Ellie's mouth ground against hers, her tongue mirroring the movements of her fingers.

Bob whimpered, feeling the first contractions of her orgasm fluttering against Ellie's fingers. Ellie felt them too, and immediately pulled her hand out, making Bob moan in dismay.

"Oh, no, I haven't finished with you yet," Ellie said, looking deep into Bob's vulnerable brown eyes. "By the time I've finished with you, you won't be in any doubt, ever again, about whether I find you desirable."

She thrust her wet fingers into Bob's mouth. "Clean them."

Helplessly, Bob laved the sticky fingers with her tongue, tasting the flavor of her own arousal.

"Good girl," breathed Ellie, then grasped Bob's knickers, tore them off her and pulled her legs apart, positioning herself between them.

Mercilessly she surveyed Bob's pussy, and then lightly stroked the lips apart to expose her fully. Bob gasped.

Ellie looked up fiercely. "I won't ever allow you to hide your beautiful body from me again. Understood?"

"Y-yes."

"You have a beautiful body. Say it."

For a second, Bob froze, and then whispered, "I have a beautiful body."

Ellie's eyes narrowed. She leaned forward to look into Bob's eyes, her hips pressing Bob's down. "Louder," she said, moving so that her pussy rubbed against Bob's.

Bob groaned. "I have a beautiful body."

Catching hold of her chin with firm fingers, Ellie held Bob's head and forced her to look into her eyes. Deliberately, she circled her hips against Bob's wet mound. Bob's eyes pleaded, even as she arched helplessly, desperately seeking release.

"Now shout it," Ellie said implacably.

"I can't!"

"Do it, Bob!"

Bob sobbed once and then, as if a great weight was lifted from her shoulders, she suddenly arched and shouted, "I have a beautiful body, I have a beautiful body, I have a beautiful body, Ellie, please, please..."

Moving fast, Ellie pulled back and parted Bob's legs with rough hands, pressing her mouth to the soaking pussy.

"Fuck!"

Suddenly Ellie found herself lifted and turned so that she was on top of Bob, sitting astride her face. Without warning, she felt Bob's fingers slide into her, even as Bob's warm tongue slid across her clit. She bucked, but Bob was ready for her, grabbing her hip and holding her in place.

But even as sensation billowed through her, she knew that what she wanted more than anything was the taste of Bob's pussy.

"Bend your legs. I want to taste you, too."

With a muffled groan, Bob did as she was told, raising her hips so that Ellie could lean forward to take her pussy in her mouth. Ellie gasped as Bob squirmed. The scent and softness and sheer beauty of Bob's form was overwhelming.

As she licked Bob's clit with wide, deep strokes she pressed her fingers firmly into her, and then started to move her fingers in time with her tongue.

Bob arched, releasing her hold on Ellie's clit momentarily to cry out. Her hips writhed. "Ellie please, baby, please..."

Ellie swept her tongue around Bob's clit, then said, tauntingly, "Please what?

"Please Ellie, please..."

"Please what?"

"Please let me come!"

Even as she said it, Ellie pressed her mouth over Bob's beautiful pussy, sucking hard and swirling her tongue around the little bud. Inside, her fingers sped up, and on pure instinct, Ellie slid a firm thumb straight into Bob's ass. She felt Bob's body go rigid, and then suddenly she was convulsing, a thousand tiny contractions fluttering around Ellie's mouth and fingers.

At the same moment, Bob grabbed Ellie's hips, drew her swollen clit into her mouth, and sucked hard. With no warning at all, Ellie exploded, grinding her soaking pussy against Bob's face as her orgasm flooded through her.

Afterward they lay together, a sated tangle of exhausted, satisfied bodies. Ellie leaned over to kiss Bob. "So, do you still think I might not find you desirable?"

Bob looked into Ellie's beautiful eyes. She had been right, she thought, absently. They did darken when she was aroused. Right now they were the most intense shade of violet she'd ever seen. She swallowed. "Sweetheart, you made your point. Wonderfully. So much for you being a rubbish lover."

Ellie grinned. "You and your sexy body inspired me to great things."

"You were great, all right. But what about you? How did you find your first time loving a woman?"

"The best night of my life. But..."

"But what?"

"But I'll never remember it as my first night loving a woman."

"You won't?"

"No." She bent down and kissed Bob's warm lips. "I'll remember it forever as my first night loving you."

HOT PANTS

Jen Cross

When I think of lust, I think of four-inch Mary Jane platforms, all black patent leather and white piping tracing the edges, being worn by a girl with the longest damn legs you ever saw—calves that curved around, butter smooth, settled over with a fine layer of gold hair, thighs like the long thunder rolling through a hot July night, and the tightest pair of hot pants you ever did see, cupped like not even second skin but first around her fleshy rump. The kinda girl who her friends say (the sharp, skinny ones at least) shouldn't exactly be wearing hot pants anyway cuz look at how her butt keeps pushing out from under the shimmery material, all sweet and jiggly and needing just and exactly the sort of attention I could be giving to it. Yeah, these cold nights up here in Detroit when the steam heat's not working right and I can hardly get the damn stove going hot enough to put some warmth into my too-tight studio, all I can do is think on Shirleen in those near-carnivorous hot pants, and how she let me in 'em just that one Christmas before I left.

* * *

Near the whole time I'd been in Atlanta, Shirleen's butt had
been firmly planted in the stony possession of her butch, Zeke.
They'd been together far back as anyone I'd met could remember,
and still she'd suddenly gaze at Z, turn those big dark-green
pools onto Zeke's tired, sweltery face with the kind of need that
you'd expect to see from newlyweds, or really skillful whores,
maybe. Zeke'd sling an arm across Shirleen's soft, broad shoulders, cop a long, possessive feel, lock eyes with one butch or
another, whoever she thought maybe had been taking one too
many tequila-glazed trips up and down Shirl's impossibly long
gams, and more often than not it'd be me Zeke'd be glaring at.
Then she'd drain her beer, stand up, reach back for her girl and
whisk Shirleen out to her Harley, with a sharp crack on the butt
and a *Well, then, come on, girl—let's get to it.* Shirleen'd grin
wide and proud and I'd sometimes think I could smell her ache
all the way across the smoky flats of the bar: somethin' steamy
and pungent and wet and quick as sea spray tracing its long,
lingering way over beach grass back home.

The night they broke up was epic, the kinda tale that gets told
at dyke bars for years, gets passed off as "Lesbian Herstory"
when it's actually just plain pain and sorrow and shamefaced
loss. Zeke went away the Sunday before solstice, no one knew
exactly where, leaving Shirleen with a half-emptied railroad flat
just a week before we were to celebrate the baby Jesus coming
all loud and star-shined and holy into the world. That year,
Christmas fell on a Friday, wouldn't you know it? (I mean, could
you believe it?) I packed my sweetest cock under my Levi's that
night with high hopes, a decision that led to the best and the
worst night of my short dumb life.

Her tears were just the beginning, fat and full on those red,
bossy cheeks. In the rear bathroom, the one that had a picture
of some old country-western dude on the front but had long

ago been claimed by the bar's femmes as a hideout, Shirleen was slumped, one leg propped up next to her, her platform shoe pushing her knee up near to the top of her head, and the other leg splayed out past the toilet, kicking at the door sometimes lazily, sometimes with a sharp vehemence, so she'd appear, then disappear, then appear again. From my perch at the side bar, I watched her in the mirror so it wouldn't look like I was really looking. Her friends kept wandering toward the john with helpful expressions on their faces, hands outstretched like they were gonna lift her up and get her cleaned off, make everything pretty again. But she swung her bottle of Cap'n Morgan at 'em (don't ask me how the bartender let her get in with that; but then, a heartbroken femme is hardly something any butch wants to tangle with, right?) and she growled real mean like I'd never heard her do before. Even from across the bar and with her half sunk into shadow, I could see the deep dark stains under her eyes. Her sorrow was so heavy it'd pushed her down to the cool concrete floor.

Soon enough, though, Shirleen stopped bouncing at the door with her one foot, shifted her leg out so she could hold it open and met my gaze. Something feral was in those eyes and I blushed hard, folded myself over my beer and tried to look away. But it'd been too long that I'd been wanting her and something throbbed itself awake in me at having her finally return my stare that way. When I peeked again into the mirror, there she was still staring, holding out a lifeline or a bridge or something. When I put my feet on the floor and pushed back my bar stool, I was careful not to look at the bartender, or at any of Shirleen's friends cluttering up the edge of the dance floor like a bunch of chickens. I tried to make myself walk steady and slow and Shirleen just got bigger and bigger and more and more real till there I was at the door. I waited till she pulled back her door-bouncing leg, like an invitation. Then I stepped into the bathroom, yanked the door shut behind me, and there I was alone in the dark with Shirleen.

I wanted there to be music around the corner from where we were about to sin so bad, about to violate every rule in the dyke handbook except for the one that says take what joy you can find where you can find it 'cause the rest of the days are gonna be hard enough. All I wanted from her was just one of the looks she used to give Zeke, that heavy openness that tells an entire room of hard-hearted and hurting women that tenderness is still possible, that tells us that there's still the possibility of someone out there who'd open their love and their arms to us in the same soft way.

But Shirleen wasn't soft that night. Her eyes were catlike in the dark and I could feel sparks erupting between us, glinting up the tiny room in a way that wouldn't help me find her bra strap but did let me know that we weren't exactly alone. She held a hand up to me, which I managed to feel, and I helped her wriggle up to a standing position. She wobbled, swaying a little where I set her against the wall, and she kept a hand on my shoulder for balance, which had me feeling like morning was rising up somewhere deep in my chest.

Someone started pounding on the door immediately—her friends, I guess, afraid she was making some big mistake. But Shirleen had reached around me and pushed that button lock with her thumb, flickering her other four fingers across my waist and then back to rest at my belly after.

"Shirleen, honey, girl, come out of there—you don't want to do this, really, d'you? Shirl? Honey?" her friends' voices pleaded through the door like bells on a late Sunday morning across a tired, crowded square. But oh, it was too early for Sunday morning yet. Shirleen reached up and pulled down the string tied to the single bare bulb above the sink mirror, and, holding my eyes in that sudden brash bright, not even blinking once but letting her wide-open, dark-green, deeply lidded and heavily mussed gaze hold me pinned to the spot, she said, "Go home, Carla Jo. I'm taking care of things my own way."

"Shirleen, please. Don't you remember...?" Shirleen squinted just a hair and interrupted her friend. "Carla Jo, girl, I mean it. Leave me alone."

"Goddamnit, Shirleen." But then the door voice went quiet, though my heart thudded so loud against my breastbone I thought for sure Carla Jo had changed her mind and come back to plead with Shirl some more.

Shirleen raised the hand still holding onto the bottle of rum and tapped her knuckles to my chest.

"Georgie, Georgie," she whispered. "What're we doin' here?" In the quiet that lengthened after she spoke, I could tell she really wanted an answer.

I wanted so bad to give her the right answer.

"Takin' care of you, Shirleen." And when her eyes flashed dark, I added, "I mean, if you'll let me."

It seemed her cheeks went a bit pinker for a moment and her eyes filled. "Been wantin' to take care of me for a long time, ain't you, Georgie?"

My mouth went dry. I just nodded.

The tears spilled out over her cheeks in great streams and she shoved me back so she could take another swig from her bottle. I caught the bottle at her mouth, gently pulled her fingers from the neck, set it down.

"I could, Shirleen. I mean it. If you let me, I could be so good to you, better, even—"

Didn't feel her hand move, just felt the sting deep at my cheek. "Better than what, Georgie?" She looked all the sudden just about ready to kill me. She rubbed her hands together, soothing the one that struck me.

"Better than anyone." I raised my hand, hesitated, then used my thumb to smooth the tears off her cheeks, cupping her head then, so thick with the desire to lay my mouth to hers that my knees were unsteady.

"Please, Shirleen," I said as she draped her arm over my shoulder and let her fingers start to play in my hair, sending shudders so hard down my back that I thought for sure she'd be able to feel them. But her gaze was unreadable, like she wore a veil over that wide-open moon face. Her gold hair, usually pulled tight and neat up into fat, juicy Marilyn Monroe–type curls, hung in shallow waves to just above her drooping shoulders. I ached to put my hands into it.

Shirleen tilted her head just a touch, tightened her grip on the back of my neck and said, pulling me to her, "Well, come on then, Georgie. Let's get to it. Show me. Show me what you been wantin' all this long time you been watchin' me."

It was all I could do not to smash my whole self into her all at one time. I felt like a thirteen-year-old kid, just desperate and shivery and plain. I set my mouth to hers, gentle and sweet, put just a little suckle behind the kiss to make her gasp. It surprised the hell outta me, though, when she did, and my eyes flew open only to meet her own shock looking right back up into me.

"Oh go ahead, Georgie. Do that again." Her lips moved, lush against my own. We stood there for a while, me cocked and ready, all denim jacket and work boots, setting what I thought was some kind of protective frame over her wet sorrow. She clung more fiercely to me with every kiss and, so slow, I let myself into her, finally tangling my fingers in that fine hair, stroking down her broad back, leaving gentle touches on her cheek. Every new touch brought that gasp back out, the sharp pull of air over both our lips, how she took my breath for her own in those moments of surprise.

"You got some other good stuff for me, Georgie?" she asked.

"Oh, Shirleen, I got just about anything you want—"

She gave a sharp laugh at that, covering it over with some-thing kind when she saw my reaction. She put her palm to my cheek and caressed it. "Oh, 'course, I know you do, baby."

She wore, as always, a tight cutoff shirt and those hot pants, behind which her butt swelled like morning sunlight. Shirleen took my hand from where I clutched up in her curls and pressed down along her body, against every curve, all the way to her butt. "Go on ahead, Georgie. Please? Ain't this what you've been waitin' for?"

I pulled her to me, groaned into her shoulder, and let both of my hands fall to cup that perfect, pendulous ass. Shirleen ground up into my crotch and she let out that kind of low growl again. "Oh no, baby, what's that? Shirleen got you that worked up already?"

Trying not to jut and jab my hips out at her, I moaned, "You know you do, honey."

Shirleen shoved me off her then, and under the vicious yellow light of that one bulb, gave me the show of my very life. With a short rip, she yanked down the zipper of those short shorts, then rocked side to side, just to work 'em down over her full hips. I didn't know what to do with my hands, kept clenching and unclenching, as the tiny room filled with the smell of her, so much sharper than I'd imagined, a little tangy, with that smell of some kind of lemon lotion she must've worn. The blonde fur around her pussy was trimmed into short curls and she let me look just a few seconds before she turned round and gave me what I'd been aching so long for, that fine round butt, thick and plain, just there, in front of me. She had to brace herself against the wall to get the shorts over first one of her Mary Janes, then the other, working the material over legs held at awkward, drunken angles. When she'd tossed the shorts to the same corner as the rum bottle, she scooted her booty up onto the cabinet that held the sink (the owners had obviously thought of just this eventuality occurring in their humblest room, and wanted to avoid having to replace sink after sink) and then shifted her thighs open, showing me the fine pearly pink skin within.

I started to go to my knees, wanting to fill my face with Shirleen's pussy, but she caught my shirt in her hand, pulling me toward her. "No, please, Georgie, not that—just fuck me, darlin'."

I could've come right then, but I wanted to wait till she hollered those words in my ear. She loosed her hold on my shirt, let her hands fall to my jeans and fumbled with the snap and zipper, releasing the cock I hadn't used since, well, since a long, long time before.

Shirleen took one of my hands then, spit into it, then wiped the palm around the shaft and slicked my hand back and forth like she was helping me jerk off. My hips rocked forward into the motion, near involuntarily, and she chuckled a little.

"Don't lose track of me now, Georgie boy," she said, and let go so she could hold her reddening lips open for me to enter. I led the cock gently, and fit what sugar I could into her bowl. "Oh god, Georgie. Please, now, come on..."

I could hardly believe I was where I was, doing what I was doing. The very air around me turned to Shirleen, filling with the smell of her, and she wrapped those crazy, thick long legs around my hips as I rocked and rocked and rocked into her. I set one hand at her ass, pulling it hard and in, put my other palm flat to the wall for balance.

Shirleen came easy, like surprise shock waves. Her thighs tightened around me, then relaxed, dropped off and hung loose around the sink. She dug at my back, clawing at my T-shirt, and let me paw at her breasts, and suckle at her sweet neckline and soft open throat. Then she tightened her legs again, and started over.

By the time we were done, I had lifted her up, turned her around and fitted myself back into her from behind. She'd bent down and propped herself up on her elbows—she had to bend her knees some so I could get in since she was so tall in those goddamn shoes—and she moaned like gangbusters. I'd hitched my hands around her hips, was rocking and fucking my way toward coming good and hard into her. Then I caught sight of Shirleen's face in the mirror.

She'd dropped her eyes and was crying again. I hadn't, of course, been able to hear the keening in her cries. I froze, couldn't bring myself to pull out and away from her body but couldn't keep on going either.

"It was 'cause of you, Georgie—'cause of you that Zeke left. Said the way you looked at me, couldn't be I'd never let you do me." She sniffed, used one hand to brush at her eyes, smearing mascara further.

"I told her so many times that it was nothin', you was just lookin' like the rest, but she said there was somethin' different. Somethin' different."

The shame was so thick in my throat I couldn't imagine ever moving again. She sobbed around her words. "I said you understood the way things were, but she said maybe I didn't understand. I said you'd never go for another butch's woman, Georgie."

If my cock could've gone limp, it would've. I slipped out of her pussy just as easy as pie and couldn't breathe anymore. Shirleen, for her part, didn't move. Just sat there, still soaking and soft and so open, wanting much more than I could give. I didn't touch her, didn't put a hand on her. Couldn't soothe away what she was saying or who I'd shown her that I was.

All around us the smell now was the indictment of her tears. "Can't you find her, Georgie? Tell her you didn't want that, tell her we never did—we never did."

I tucked my cock back into my drawers and then zipped up. I wanted something to cover her with, but there was nothing. Her exposure was too much for me.

She raised her eyes and met my gaze in the mirror once again, and her face fell in that instant. I had backed away from her, as far as I could get. Her eyes sharpened to flint and she watched me open the door a hair, with her still bent and offering, there at the sink. I slipped out, shut the door and listened again to her sobs.

It seemed like the whole bar (near empty now and still) was glaring at me, most especially Shirleen's best friend Carla Jo and her butch, the bartender, Azele. I stopped at the bar for a second to gather my jacket and Azele came over to me with a shot of bourbon, and let me throw it back. "You're gonna have to go, Georgie—you know that, right?"

I knew. I went. And still and now, all the way up here in the frozen North—even jerking off in my little twin bed to every part of that night except the very end, but even so not quite being able to come—I know. I'm still leaving. I can't get far enough away.

BIKE PEDAL.
EMPANADAS.
AND WHISKEY.

Aimee Herman

I am going to try to find an adjective. One I've never used before, which may be difficult since I tend to use the same ones. And for the purpose of our conversation, I will call this person I'm trying to describe Q. I am going to need you to get comfortable. Order your drink now, so that when you take your last sip, the waiter will already know what you want and there will be no interruption. What's that? Yes, it is quite loud in here, but this seemed like the best table and I do like the ambiance. Thickly painted women stuck inside these giant canvases. That one over there. Look. That one's cleavage looks as though it's a spill from the neck down. Don't you think? Okay, good. You've got your whiskey and I've got mine.

The start of this isn't so romantic. I was in a bike shop in Brooklyn on Franklin Avenue. Yes, that new one. And I was with my lover who had a busted pedal and needed a replacement. Inhale for a moment. Oh, take your sip and then inhale. Yes. Imagine this shop with scents of tires and oil. Now breathe in deeper because my lover interrupted these smells with his

face. He still reeked of my cunt. He hadn't brought his cock
the night before when he came over, so he preferred to leave
his clothes on. I was able to persuade him out of his pants and I
imagined his cock into me. I was nude as I often am when I am
home. He lifted me and I wrapped my thighs around him as
though my legs were fan blades whipping at his hips. He didn't
throw me onto the bed; this isn't a movie. It was a careful drop.
He did not take the time to kiss my inner thighs or my belly or
even my mouth. He just sucked out the sweat of my bush and
dug his tongue into me.

Damn, this whiskey is good. I don't even want to be gentle
with it, you know? Where was I? So, we are in the bike shop.
He is talking to the mechanic about his pedal, asking him to
look at the alignment as well. I was walking around, my cunt
still sore, wishing we hadn't left my apartment, and then I saw
Q. Here is where the proper adjective has to come into play.
Imagine a mellifluous voice. And face. And…well, everything.
Are you with me? Do you see this? Can you picture this? Okay.
This isn't Q. This one was more like aluminum. You know
when you messily remove the metallic-like casing on the top of
a wine bottle? It's a bit sharp. It bends, but it can also cut. This
is Q. There was no melody or rhythm to Q's face. It was more
like grit. Fleshy, thick gravel. Q was wearing jeans, denim that
just hung like a hard waterfall plunging from hips. There was
a gathering at the bum and don't worry, I searched for it. I
stared. And my stare was unapologetic. It was guiltless. My
stare did not care that I had just been fucked by my lover who
had lustful rage in his fingers from yesterday's T shot. My stare
had no remorse for the fact that just a few feet away my lover
was arguing about price with the mechanic while I wondered
how I could get this human in denim, with shadowed cheek-
bones, to leave with me but not go too far. Walk up Park to
where that abandoned building is. I think there was a fire there

many years ago. And I'd slip my hands down Q's pants. Not even unbutton. Everything would remain on us because it is only two in the afternoon. It isn't nighttime. There is plenty of sun breathing out its energy at us still. And I'd search out Q's erection.

Wait. What did you just order? Yeah, I'll have one of those too. This booze is making me so slippery. Okay. So, my fingers would be wrapped around whatever is in Q's pants. And by the look of things in that bike shop, Q was packing. And Q would aggressively put a hand right into my pants, and notice I was packing as well. It was my soft cock, the one I wore just for me, but it could still be played with, even in its pliability.

Shit, do you see who that is? Fuck. Alana. What do you mean you don't know who that—don't you remember last June? That stupid lesbian speed-dating event I went to? Kelly dragged me and I only went because she had been miserable because of her breakup. I can be so soft sometimes. Anyway, it was the end of the night. Alana was my last "date." I was exhausted. She wasn't exactly my type. She was covered in makeup. I could barely see the shape of her face, but she also had on these incredibly sexy stockings. I just wanted to tear them off with my teeth. As she asked me the most banal questions, I couldn't help fantasizing tying myself up, forcing away my limbs, so I could use my teeth to tear at the webbed stitching and lick her released skin. I managed to put my hand on her knee, and instruct her to slowly get up. No, I wasn't drunk. All they had was wine, and you know that has no effect on me. I said to her: I want to watch the creases on your dress slowly suction themselves to your body. Then I want you to leave. I will be behind you, I told her. She grabbed her purse, which was so small I can't imagine how she could even fit a lipstick in that thing, and she walked out. I followed close behind. We got to the end of the street and turned. I pushed my body against hers and threw my hand beneath her dress, which was the exact shade of red that her ass became by the end of the night. My fingers were inside her and—

What? No, I was gentle. I mean, I started with two fingers before I switched to four. She writhed like wind and kissed her lipstick onto me. Fuck, you know how I feel about lipstick, but it tasted so sweet. Her lips actually tasted like an ingredient. Buttery...like a croissant or something. She used her palm to press against my cunt and then she just turned all rubbery and could barely touch me. She lost it. Came all over my hand.

Where are our drinks? Didn't we order something? Anyway, sometimes nights are meant to remain as just that: one night. Somehow she got my phone number. Kelly must have given it to her; I'm pretty sure they knew each other. I am not exaggerating when I tell you that this girl texted me constantly. We went out a few times after that, but we wanted very different things. I was looking to orgasm; she was looking for a girlfriend.

Shit, I've gotten extremely off course. Bike shop. So, my lover is now paying for the new pedal and asking a bunch of questions about adding gears to his bike or something. Q is noticing my stare. Good. I still haven't named a proper adjective have I? I did? Well, here are a few more. So, Q's hair was that kind of messy that looked like it had been mashed between hands and rubbed against a bed, back and forth. I know there're hair products out there to make hair look this way, but Q's hair practically stunk of fucking.

Are you okay? Maybe we should get you some water. Or we can order those empanadas you like. They make 'em good here. Yeah, let's get two orders of those. And two more whiskeys, yeah? So, I notice my lover putting his wallet in his back pocket and heading toward me. I feel one second of guilt that I want him to leave. I want him to just walk out and forget he came with me. I can feel Q watching as my lover grabs my hips and pulls me into him. He tells me something about how much this new pedal cost. I don't care. I'm just thinking about the shape of Q and the way I want to suck out Q's tongue. Suddenly, my lover gets a phone call. He digs out his phone and answers it. I know it must be important because usually he communicates through text only. Yeah, he's one of those. And then, he motions to me that he has to go. Something about work or his mom or actually, all I cared was that he was leaving and I wasn't leaving without Q.

How about a verb? Q stumbled. It wasn't exactly a stagger. Or maybe it was. It's like the difference between print and cursive. You know, they stopped teaching cursive in schools? Shit. Anyway, Q's body was writing in cursive. These movements were squiggly and it's like each bone was speaking in a different language. No, no. Not like drunk. More like this loose, slow transition from heel to toe to wooden floorboard to air to—even though I'm pretty sure by the look of Q and knowledge of my own morning, we had both been fucked already that day, there was still hunger in us. And I swear to you I am not lying when I said to Q: leave with me. And there was absolutely no hesitation as Q grabbed a bike and we literally left. What? No, I couldn't take Q home with me. As smutty as I can be, my bed is only for my lover. I didn't even think about asking to go to Q's place. Instead, we walked the four or so blocks to that bar you and I went to that time for Reyna's birthday. They have those single-serving bathrooms. Fucking small. Barely big enough for one, but then there is that one that is like a suite in comparison. Big mirror on the wall. That came in handy. So we fucked and then I went home and made myself a really delicious lunch of—

What? What do you need to know? Haven't I said enough? You gonna have that last empanada? Damn, these are good. I like how they kind of burn my tongue a little and it is almost painful to swallow—okay! The thing was we were both aggressive. There was nothing soft about Q and I was right, there was definite packing. Q was taller than I am; did I mention that? I don't think I talked about height. Yeah, so Q kind of pushed my head down. Got me on my knees and just pushed cock out from that gorgeous hole built into underwear, which were bright red, by the way. Suddenly, I've got a mouthful of polyurethane cock and I am just sucking and sucking, feeling it give and stretch in my mouth. The great thing is that I can use my teeth and Q doesn't even know it. I can be clumsy and I don't have to pretend to deep-throat it, even though I totally did. I practically swallowed it. I—

You want me to stop? Oh, yeah. Let's grab another drink; I'm pretty thirsty too. I swear they water these drinks down. So, Q's back is bent toward the wall. It's scooped out. Then I just get up, pull my pants down, move my cock out of the way so I can finger myself for a minute, realize how wet I am and throw this thick cock into me. We are pressed so firmly together, I cannot believe we just met. I—no, I...what I mean is, we are just moving at a rhythm that feels—what? I'm not going to pretend it didn't feel good. I'm not—yeah, I guess something happened. I mean, my lover fucks me with his cock—actually, he has several that he uses on me, but Q's...it's like my cunt had been chiseled into the exact shape to take this one in. I know, I know what I sound like.

What? Don't compare me to Alana. Yeah, we kissed. Of course, we kissed. And it was monstrous and harsh. I'm not going to call it romantic. It was everything but that. Our mouths were greedy. And then I just...sort of...twisted around, which happened so fast, I actually lost track of everything. We were...I don't know...I felt like Q was climbing into me. I don't know how long we were in there. It doesn't matter. All I know is that I left my bones in there that day. Like several, significant bones in there in that dirty, fucking bathroom.

No, I never saw Q again. Of course, right? Isn't that how it goes? And I broke up with my lover two days later. Nothing felt right after that day. It's like...it's like my shape changed.

BENNIE

Sommer Marsden

I watched Bennie the way I did every morning. Stomping out of her house in her big work boots. She walked like she had a vendetta against the world, and the way she carried herself never failed to turn me on. She clutched a to-go mug of coffee and rooted in her deep pockets for her car keys. Every morning she did this, and every morning I enjoyed the ritual.

I sat inside my apartment, watching her as I drank from my Snoopy mug. My computer whirred gently and my freelance work waited and yet...I watched her.

I had this fantasy, had had it for ages, where she'd stalk over here instead of to her car. She'd rap on the door hard enough to make me jump instead of root for her keys. She'd ask me out on a date instead of driving off to work.

It had yet to happen. Would probably never happen. But I had the fantasy anyway. It went on from there. Her coming to pick me up for said date in her black fitted trousers and her leather vest. The one she only wore to special events. Semi-casual, she'd once laughed when I complimented her on it. I'd been getting the mail, she'd been heading out for the night.

I'd blushed as if I'd asked her to drop to her knees and go down on me instead of complimenting her outfit. It had taken everything in me to do it and yet I'd forced myself. Then I'd watched her pull away in her '66 Mustang coupe—white to her almost consistently black ensembles. After she'd gone, I'd damn near staggered into the house, dropped to the sofa, shoved my hand into my panties and gotten myself off, not once, but twice. Just remembering her clear blue eyes on me and the way she'd laughed.

It made me want to kiss her, that laugh. It made me want to fuck.

I'd let the curtain drop so when the doorbell rang I damn near swallowed my own tongue. A peek through the window showed me Bennie, and I found my feet had disappeared on me. I couldn't feel them at all. Nor my lips. My face was on its way to being numb as well, but I forced my hands to work the lock and then turn the doorknob.

"Hey, hi," I stammered. "What's up, Bennie?"

She had no idea. She was clueless. She didn't know that as we stood there I was wet inside my panties, frantic and nervous inside my stomach.

"Car," she growled. "Won't start. And…" She patted her pocket and a clicking sound arose. "Phone's dead. You'd think I would remember to charge it, right? I have no home line." She stared at me.

And? And? My mind scrambled for words. Finally, she did that little half-smile thing of hers that always made me want to drop to my knees and beg her to notice me. She ran a hand through her close-cropped dark hair and said, "So…Ava…"

"Yes?" Damn if I didn't sound breathless. It was mortifying.

"Can I use your phone to call a tow?"

My heart kicked in my chest, hard. I realized my stupidity.

How silly I must have looked. "Of course!" I chirped. "I'm so sorry. Clearly I need more coffee." I was babbling as I hurried to the kitchen to grab the portable home line. My cell was dead too, so that made us two for two in the dead cell department.

When I turned she had come in right behind me. Standing so close to me, I could see the green striations around the pupils in her blue eyes. I could smell some sandalwood scent on her skin and the clean generic smell of shampoo and soap. I could see up close what those lips looked like in that little twist of a half smile.

She took the phone from me and her fingers brushed my hand. I jolted and then tittered nervously when she noticed.

"I didn't hear you come," I said. Then caught my words and had enough presence of mind to feel my cheeks flame red in an instant.

"Oh, you would." She laughed. "Thanks."

She punched in a number that she seemed to know by heart and turned her back to me. "Tony, it's Bennie. The Mustang. Yeah. Again. I thought you fixed that shit. I mean, come on—yeah, okay, forty-five minutes."

She hung up the phone and shook her head. "Fucking mechanics. Thanks, Ava. I'll go wait out by the ca—"

"Have some coffee," I blurted. "It's cold and…"

I don't want you to go.

But I didn't finish. I swallowed hard waiting for her decision.

She cocked her head and smiled again. When she stuck her hands in her pockets the long, thin silver chain that went from her wallet to her belt loop swayed. More than once I'd imagined that chain wound around my wrists as Bennie did things to me. Dirty things. Good things. Whatever she damn well pleased.

She caught me watching that chain. She tapped the toe of her boot on my black and white linoleum floor. When she smiled this time my stomach dropped. That was the smile of a predator. The knowledge that she'd get whatever she wanted, the pleasure from that knowledge...they were written all over her face. I didn't know whether to feel excited as opposed to afraid.

I was both. It was magnificent.

"Why don't you pour me some coffee," she said slowly.

I hurried to do it but she reached out and grabbed my wrist before I could get too far. I gasped, turned to face her, not sure what was going to happen. "I wasn't done, Ava."

"Sorry," I stammered. A wet, thick ache had taken up residence inside me. I pictured her hands on me. Her fingers in me. Her mouth on me. My own mouth had gone dry.

"While you're pouring me that coffee, tell me what you were just thinking. Just now. Looking at me."

"At you? I..." Maybe I was about to deny it all, I thought. Maybe my embarrassment would get the better of me.

"When you were looking at my wallet chain. I want to know. And don't lie," she said, squeezing my wrist hard enough to make my pulse thump wickedly. "I'll know if you lie."

I believed her.

"I can't," I said. I'd lusted after her for over two years but our interactions had been kept to softly shouted greetings, the occasional wave, an exchanged bottle of booze at Christmas. I'd picked up her mail for her when she'd been away and she'd gotten mine for me but never...

"You can. Tell me."

If I told her she'd know everything. How long, how bad, how much the want was.

She squeezed my wrist again and my pulse struggled against the press of her fingers.

"I was thinking...I was thinking," I started again, trying to not faint. "About you wrapping my wrists in that chain."

I felt like I might faint. I didn't realize I wasn't breathing until Bennie said, "Breathe."

I inhaled deeply and my head stopped swimming.

"Better?" she asked. Her thumb was sweeping back and forth over my skin.

"Better," I said.

"So you finally get the nerve to talk to me, I mean really talk to me," she said. "And you confess light bondage fantasies. You're a trip, Ava." She chuckled and something inside me melted like hot caramel.

"I...yes. I guess so. I had no idea you...knew," I finished weakly. Looking at my feet. Unable to meet her blue gaze.

I heard the chain jingle against itself while I continued to stare—fascinated—at her boots. Her wallet hit the table with a muffled leather thud. And then as I watched—and for a moment I feared I was hallucinating—she wound the thin silver chain around my wrists.

I sighed. It was the most honest sound I'd ever made. The sound of a person getting what she wanted from the person she wanted. The sound of satisfaction.

When my wrists were bound in front of me, my robe hung partly open and my bare knees started to tremble from the chill of the November morning.

"What's next?" she asked, cocking an eyebrow. She leaned against the breakfast bar and watched me.

I stared down at my bound wrists as if they had all the answers. "I..."

She waited. After a minute or two of silence she said. "You? What, Ava?"

"I don't know," I confessed. "What happened next was always up to you. You were in charge. Are," I corrected. "Are in charge."

She inclined her head slowly, a thoughtful kind of nod. "I see. So whatever I want?" Her eyes were brighter, her smile wider. For some reason I felt like Little Red before the wolf.

"I've wanted you for a long time," she said softly.

I startled. "You did? Why didn't you...but you had to know that I..." I shook my head. "Words aren't my friend right now."

"Why didn't I ask you out?" she asked, closing the distance between us.

"Yes." The air was leaving the room the closer she got.

"Because you're such a nice girl," she said. She accented the word nice and simultaneously reached for me. Bennie trapped my nipple between her finger and thumb. She squeezed with increasing pressure through my satin nightgown. "And I'm not really a nice guy."

"You're nice," I said to her. "You are."

"I'm rough around the edges," she said. Her fingers moved laterally and she trapped my other nipple, giving it the same treatment. The pain of it made me grit my teeth but my cunt, oh, my cunt was gloriously drenched.

Bennie leaned in and kissed me. It was short but staggering. Her mouth a hot, insistent force moving against mine. Then she dragged her teeth none too gently down my throat until I sobbed. She released my nipple and the blood flowing back into that tender flesh was breathtaking.

"Get on your knees, Ava. If I get whatever I want, then I want what's been in my head for the last two years."

My hair tumbled around my shoulders, the pin having fallen out. My knees hit the cool kitchen floor. She held my elbow to make sure I didn't fall. I was shaking. My mind racing. I knelt there as she undid her silver belt buckle and slid the leather from her belt loops. She dangled it in front of me.

"One day, if today goes well, maybe you and my belt can get acquainted. Something tells me," she glanced conspicuously at her wallet chain around my wrist, "that you wouldn't mind getting to feel the stripes from this belt on your skin."

My shaking turned to full-on tremors. My panties were

soaked and my breath was short in my lungs. "I wouldn't," I said, barely above a whisper. "What does that make me to you, Bennie?" I asked, forcing myself to be brave. I was curious. I wanted to know.

She smiled. "It makes you honest, Ava," she said, stroking my cheek. "Now open your mouth. You're going to get me off." Then she unzipped her pants and pushed them down. Beneath the black fabric she was bare, her pubic hair close cut and neat.

She grabbed the back of my head and shoved my face between her legs. She was rough about it and it had me on the verge of toppling over. So many times I'd run bittersweet scenarios in my head. Tumultuous but hot sex with Bennie and here we were and it was...perfect.

I did what she wanted. I licked and sucked and nudged her clit with my tongue. It was fairly large and easy to target, which was good because I was so nervous my knees were quite literally knocking together as I knelt there.

"Good mouth," she laughed softly. She gripped my hair in her strong hand and tugged hard enough to bring tears to my eyes. A startled noise escaped me. She tugged again and I moaned, grinding my face, my lips, my tongue into her. She was sweet and musky and the sandalwood she wore blended with the natural scent of her. It filled my nose and blotted out the world.

Bennie grunted, thrusting her pelvis forward and meeting my mouth roughly. I kept at it, licking and sucking and drinking her in. My hands were bound or I would have touched her. I settled for letting my fingers stroke the skin below her knee. It was all I could reach but I wanted to touch her.

Somehow that did it for her. She swore once, followed it with "Christ!" and gripped my head in her hands. The world grew muffled because she was covering my ears. But I still heard her cries as she came. My mouth grew slick with her juices and I tried to gather every last drop.

Two years of wet waking dreams about Bennie and here we were, thanks to her aging Mustang and a crappy mechanic, apparently.

"Stand up, stand up," she growled. She helped lift me from the floor with her hand on my elbow. But once I was up, she slammed me back against the breakfast bar hard enough to drive the air out of me. I gasped when she yanked the tie on my robe, parted it fully and pushed her hands up under my nightgown. Her hand yanked hard and my panties were dragged down my thighs. When her hands were hot on my bare skin, I heard myself whimper.

Bennie kissed me and I gave myself over to it completely. My whole body bending to hers, my mind racing, wishing, begging for her to touch me.

She stroked my hips slowly as if she were petting me. "Bennie…" I whispered.

She kissed me again. Her tongue insistent on mine. "Say it," she said.

"Say what?" I asked. Then her tongue was in my mouth again, and I was returning her kiss. Swooning under its influence.

"Tell me what you want. You were brave, Ava. You told me about the chain. Now what?" She dragged her tongue over my lips, tasting herself there. She smiled at me, and my stomach clenched.

"I want you to…" I bit my bottom lip. She watched me.

"Say it. You can do it, Ava."

"I want you…" I looked her in the eye. It undid me. The clear blue gaze. The honest curiosity there. "Oh god, Bennie. Please. Please just touch me. Please just make me come," I said.

She grinned. Her pale-pink lips curving into a look of pure joy. But her blue eyes had grown hooded with arousal. A single lock of dark hair had fallen across her brow and it gave her a rakish appearance. "That's all you had to say, doll."

Her hands slid up the tops of my thighs. She spread her fingers so more of my skin was stimulated. I whimpered. The tips of her thumbs nearly met on my bare mound. That sensation, so close to where I wanted it, was maddening.

She moved her fingers back and forth, back and forth over my skin until I was panting. Gasping for air. Reaching for oxygen.

She slid her thumbs a little higher and then used them to spread my lips. Bowing from her waist exactly, Bennie blew on my clit. I jumped. Mewled.

"Such a good girl. I think after two long years…" *Blow, blow.* Air feathered across my tenderest, hottest skin. All the while her thumbs kept me spread, awakening nerve endings that came alive under the pressure. "You deserve a good orgasm."

She leaned in, still bent impossibly at the waist. How did she manage such a perfect posture? Her tongue snaked out and sliced wetly across my clitoris.

"Bennie…" I exhaled.

"Yes, Ava?" Another drag of her tongue and my hips shot forward roughly. A sudden involuntarily motion.

"Please," I said again. Desperate now. Needy beyond comprehension. I wanted this to last forever and yet I wanted her to put me out of my misery.

She dropped to her knees and peeled my pussy lips back farther. I clutched my bound hands between my breasts so I could watch her. Watch her push her face to my cunt. Watch her head moving as she licked me. Her hair was cut so close in some spots I could see her scalp shining white beneath. I studied the buzzed nape, clean and crisp as if she'd just been to the barbershop. I studied her strong shoulders and back inside her gray-and-white-striped button-down as she ate me. As pleasure flooded me and orgasm approached, I drank her in. The fact that she was in here. On her knees getting me off. And that the taste of her was still on my lips.

"Sweet. I knew it," she said, glancing up at me. Her gaze sly and beyond sexy.

Her fingers drove into me and my knees dipped. I pressed against the breakfast bar to keep from falling on my ass. She added a third finger, filling me, stretching me until I felt as if might shatter apart in front of her.

"Come for me, Ava. After all this damn time, give it to me."

She sucked my clit harder than before. The feel of her drawing on me with her mouth broke my last bit of resolve. My bound hands came down atop her head, her brown hair soft under my fingers. I bucked my hips, let my head fall back and came. She just kept licking and I just kept coming. It unwound from me, a long golden ribbon of pleasure that seemed to fill my entire body.

"Bennie," I said, and blushed. I realized I'd waited two years to say that aloud. To her. While we fucked.

Outside there was a rapid-fire string of beeps and she chuckled, wiping her mouth with the back of her hand. She stood, put herself back together and retrieved her wallet. After unwinding her chain from my wrist she hooked it back to her belt loop. When she was all neatened up and complete—just the way she'd walked in—she kissed me. Wrapping her hand in my hair to anchor me as she pushed her tongue against mine, her lips restless and seeking.

"I'll be back after work. To take you out. Maybe we can talk. Eat. Get to know a few more things about each other before we do that again."

I nodded, the heat in my cheeks still blazing strong. "Okay."

"But don't worry," she said, heading toward the door. She opened it and waved to whoever was out waiting for her by the Mustang.

"Worry about what?" I blurted. I pulled my robe tight around me. I studied the pretty pattern of her chain on my skin.

"Don't worry," she said, winking. The cold November air rippled her short hair. It made me shiver. "We'll be doing that again."

I nodded, chewing my lower lip again. "Good."

"And more, Ava," she said, pulling the door after her as she left.

"And more," I echoed, smiling.

THE MEASURE OF A MAN

Victoria Janssen

Jerusha Pettifer desperately needed this position.

He checked the fall of his breeches to make sure everything was fastened and in place, smoothed a hand over his waistcoat and twitched his cravat, hoping the shabby shirt beneath wasn't obvious. He couldn't do anything about his age, or his face. He bit the inside of his cheek, hard; the momentary pain distracted, then calmed him. He lifted his gloved hand to the knocker and rapped.

Ten minutes later, he sat in a sober library, gaping at the woman of the house and wondering if he should suddenly pretend to have another appointment.

Mrs. Lambert said calmly, "Your expression, Mr. Pettifer! So droll. You are suspicious of our desires? Tell me what you think. What you *truly* think." The words rolled from her mouth rich and inflected as an actor's, in direct contrast to her staid afternoon gown, lavishly trimmed in lace that matched the cap over her graying red hair. When she stopped speaking, Jerusha found himself wishing she would say something else. Anything else.

The other woman in the room, introduced to him only as
Lilias, licked her lips. She had been the first clue these women
were not looking for an ordinary footman. She lounged on a
settee in the corner, wearing a man's silken banyan and, so far
as he could tell, nothing else. He'd been trying very hard not to
imagine that nothing else, nor to imagine what she'd been up to
before he'd arrived, and failing miserably.

A recklessness he'd never felt before tingled through his
muscles. "Yes, I am suspicious," he said. He touched his crooked
nose, indicated his rough brawniness. "A man like me?" Bluntly,
he added, "Going through the Registry to find yourself a man-
whore, you could've found a lot younger and prettier."

The silence seemed to vibrate.

He'd been an idiot. He needed a position, and he needed it
now. If he didn't get a position, and a well-paying one... He
should have...hell, what should he have said? Would they be
worrying he was planning to blackmail them?

Lilias smiled. Though her striking face was barely lined, her
Brutus-cropped hair matched the banyan's gleaming silver fabric
and appeared just as thick and silky-soft. Her eyes were green
as the emerald rope binding the loose robe close to her slender
waist. All of that, however, was as nothing compared to the glory
of her curving bosom and round bottom. She said, "We want a
man like you. Honest in his dealings. Honest in his pleasures."

Her eyes and voice were forthright like an army officer's.
It had been a long time since anyone had spoken to him like
that. He needed the money, and he admitted to himself that he
wanted Lilias, wanted to tangle his hands in her thick hair and
bury his face in her lush bosom. He wanted to take this chance,
no matter the risks to his future. "You'd better have me, then."

Mrs. Lambert smiled. No, she grinned. "There! We do plan
to 'have you,' Mr. Pettifer. In every possible way. If you will
accept our offer of employment."

Every possible way. A shiver went through him, not entirely fear. "I want five hundred pounds," he said, "payable tomorrow morning by bank draft." It was an absurd sum, but if he was going to do this, he wanted it to be more than worth it. He waited for them to refuse and have him escorted out.

Less than a half hour later, sans boots, coat and waistcoat, he lay stretched across the most massive wooden bed he'd ever seen, staring up at the inside of the gilt-framed mirrored canopy. *I should have asked for a thousand pounds. And a nice big fire in this room.*

He'd been a fool to agree to this. He'd always thought himself a steady sort, moderate in his tastes, reserved in his dealings, always careful to avoid trouble. That was how he'd gotten this far. What would they expect of him? And what would these society women do once they realized what exactly they'd bought?

The dressing room door opened, and Magdalene Lambert sauntered in, her hair wound atop her head in a knot, emphasizing her elegant bone structure. She was wearing fawn breeches with a shirt and waistcoat, her form revealed as slender and boyish, in a way that was more stirring than if she had been naked. Jerusha rolled to his side to see her better. She wasn't wearing boots; instead, her bony, pale feet dug into the imported rug with a tactile delight he could almost feel on his skin. In her male clothing, she was the most beautiful thing he had ever seen, more lovely even than Lilias.

He lifted his eyes to her face; she was smiling, faintly. "Do you like what you see, Mr. Pettifer? We would prefer you to speak honestly."

"I like your hips in those breeches," he confessed. "But I'd like to get you out of that waistcoat." She had only the faintest curve of bosom; he wanted to see if her breasts would fit within his palms.

"All in good time."

Lilias entered the room then, and Jerusha lost his breath; she was utterly, gloriously naked. His eyes traveled from her full breasts down to the swell of her hips; then he saw the arrangement of leather straps around her waist and between her legs. In her hand, she held a carved wooden cock, flanged at the base. She said, "It's not for you, Mr. Pettifer. Unless you ask me very, very nicely." Then she turned and presented the cock to Magdalene.

Jerusha propped himself on one elbow. "May I ask—"

Magdalene laid her hand, not the one holding the wooden cock, on his chest and pushed him flat. "No, you may not. Hold this." She laid the cock in his palm and, reflexively, his fingers closed over it. The wood was smooth as a well-worn banister, and warm from its contact with skin. The head had been shaped with intricate detail, including an engraved slit.

Lilias climbed onto the bed, and his attention immediately shifted to the swing of her breasts as she crawled over to him. "Put it into your mouth," she said.

"Which—which end?"

Lilias smiled, and slowly licked her lips. "Make it wet." She straddled his shins, planting her hands on his thighs. "I want it to be very wet for Magdalene. Do it well, and I will reward you." Her left hand shifted higher, just brushing the inside of his thigh. Any closer, and she would realize that he did not have a cock there, only a tightly rolled stocking.

Should he speak? Instead, he opened his mouth and slipped the wooden cock inside, sucking hard and laving it thoroughly with his tongue. His fingers wanted to caress Lilias, but she hadn't asked, and he clenched his hands in the bedclothes instead.

What would her soft flesh feel like? He'd always wondered what it would be like, to have another's warm naked flesh against his own. But he'd never been able to take that risk, not when it might mean his livelihood.

Lilias drew the cock from his mouth, slowly, caressing his cheek with her other hand. His breath caught; he slowly let it out, only to catch again as her fingers brushed, featherlight, across his lips. Lilias laid her hand on his chest and rubbed gently; then her hand stopped. "What are you wearing, Mr. Pettifer?"

He swallowed. The time had come. "Bindings," he said. "A sort of corset."

Magdalene appeared at the side of the bed. She said, "Mr. Pettifer. Are you quite healthy?"

"Aye. Just...just not a man." The words came out, but after them he couldn't breathe.

Lilias burst into laughter. Jerusha winced, but he could breathe again. Magdalene demanded, "Who sent you?"

"The agency, ma'am." Jerusha's heart pounded; he felt cold all over. "Just let me up, and I'll go. I shan't say a word, I promise, if you'll only let me go."

Lilias pressed down on his chest, still laughing, and said, "No, no! Stay! Magdalene, she must stay! This is most wonderful!"

Being called by the feminine pronoun gave Jerusha a strange feeling. "I've never been called wonderful before. Abomination, more like. And thief, for stealing honest work from men with families. But you can keep your five hundred pounds. I'll find it elsewhere."

Magdalene appeared about to speak, then stopped. "Lilias, we must discuss this."

"I'll leave," Jerusha said. "I'm sorry I deceived you. I—"

"You'll wait here," Lilias said firmly. She laid the wooden cock on the bed. "Tell me, what is your true name?"

"Jerusha Pettifer, as I said. I know it's a man's name, but my da—"

"Remain here, Jerusha. Please?"

Truth be told, he felt so weak and shaky that he didn't think he would have made it far. "Aye."

As soon as the women had departed the room, Jerusha sat up, arms clasped around upraised knees, back against the carved oaken headboard. Running would do little good. His secret might be safe with these women, but his heart would not be. Saying the words, easy as they'd spilled out, had snapped something open in his chest, leaving him tender and near bleeding. He laid his forehead on his knees and closed his eyes. If he had to walk out of this room, he would rip himself in two, half of him always yearning to reach out and touch.

He ought to have looked for a day's work down at the docks, hauling crates.

A hand rested on the back of his head, sending his heart into his throat. Lilias touched his cheek. "Jerusha. We'd like you to stay with us."

Magdalene stood just beyond, hands on hips. "This is most unusual, but then we are hardly usual ourselves. Lilias and I feel we'd be foolish to throw you into the street, when...that is, we would like to know more about you. For instance, why did you accept our offer?"

"I was curious," Jerusha admitted. "I needed the money, yes, but when I saw Lilias, I wanted...I can stay?"

"If you'll have us," Lilias said. "We thought we might go about things a little differently, if you don't mind."

Jerusha shrugged. "It makes no matter to me. I've never done this before."

"Never—?"

"Bedroom games," he explained. "Wasn't safe. Someone would find out."

Magdalene said, "But you want us."

Jerusha nodded. "If you'll have me. And you've just said you will."

Lilias sat beside him on the bed and gathered him into her arms. Her bosom was even softer and more comforting than

Jerusha's wildest imaginings. He turned his face into her throat; she smelled delicious, like fresh bread from a bakery. A moment later, the mattress dipped again as Magdalene joined them, laying a kiss against Jerusha's tangle of curls. She said, softly, "Now I know why you appealed to me so much more than the others we interviewed. I've a special fondness for bravery."

"Thank you," Jerusha said. "Thank you for not having a footman toss me out."

"You can thank us with a kiss," Lilias said. "Here, put your arms around me."

The next little while was a revelation of warmth and closeness. Jerusha found himself divested of shirt and then binding, laid flat upon the mattress and caressed by direct, knowing hands. He'd briefly felt big and awkward next to their elegant slenderness, but soon forgot it in the wonder of tangling his hands in Lilias's cropped hair while she kissed him with tongue and teeth, and the pleasantly painful ache caused by Magdalene's steady licking and sucking of his tender nipples.

Lilias sat up and stretched languorously. Her lips were swollen and red, her hair wild. She laid her hand over her cunny and moaned softly. "I thought I was in the mood to peg a man's arse, but now I find I want to be filled," she said, in a slow and deliberate tone that made Jerusha shiver. "Magdalene, do you think this harness will fit Jerusha?"

"I have another," Magdalene said. "Let me fetch it."

"You mean, you wish me to wear the cock," Jerusha said. The thought made his belly twist and his clit twinge with need. "You'll allow me to fuck you like a man?"

"Better than a man, I'd hope!" Lilias said, running her hands down Jerusha's sides, and trailing a finger around the high waist of his trousers. "Shall we have these off now?"

It wasn't so difficult after all, to strip off the last remaining layers of trousers and drawers and false cock. Magdalene

returned from the dressing room with the harness and a porce-
lain jar of ointment. They all three knelt on the massive bed
while Magdalene worked the straps into place, her fingers warm
on Jerusha's hips and arse. When she'd finished, she put her
arms around Jerusha from behind and nuzzled his neck. "You'll
like this, I think."

Lilias had removed her own harness. She dragged the wooden
cock free of her lips with a naughty popping sound and began to
grease it with the ointment. "I want you to be in me," she said.
"You'll likely need to guide it with your hand."

Magdalene cupped Jerusha's breasts in her hands. "I love to
watch," she confessed. "Later, I'll want my own pleasure, but
for now I want you to forget I'm there while you fuck Lilias."
She nibbled Jerusha's earlobe, and then licked it before removing
herself from the bed. She still wore her male clothing, now in
disarray. She selected a chair and dragged it close to the bed,
draping one of her legs over the padded arm and stroking her
cunny through her breeches. She looked like an arrogant young
lord. Jerusha's mouth watered, just looking at her.

Lilias laid the cock in Jerusha's trembling hand. "It goes in
this way," she said, arranging the flanged bottom in the harness
so it pressed, suddenly, against Jerusha's clit. Then she took his
face between her hands and kissed him messily. "Do you want
to be atop?"

In reply, Jerusha took her shoulders in his hands, pressing
her back to the mattress. She lifted one knee, cocking her leg to
the side, and held her cunny open. Her lower lips were already
shiny with a mixture of her own wetness and ointment; she
arched her hips up, asking for Jerusha's cock.

They fit well together, though Jerusha was the taller. He had
often wondered what it would be like to truly possess a cock,
and imagined himself thrusting into a woman as he brought
himself to completion. It was a different thing entirely to feel

the pressure on his clit as he angled the cock into Lilias's cunny, thrusting tentatively at first, then more firmly once the cock was deeply seated. He groaned as he rubbed his hips into hers, and the cock's flange rubbed his clit. Nearby, he heard Magdalene's answering moan, but he didn't look away from Lilias, her face flushed with passion, her eyes huge and dark as she bucked her hips into him. Her hands skidded down his back, then dug into his buttocks.

He was close to coming after only a few moments, then suddenly went over, crying out and shuddering in Lilias's arms. She hadn't come off, though, and as soon as he could he began again, this time thrusting harder, grinding into her mound until she, too, cried out and convulsed, her heart racing against his.

Magdalene helped to remove the cock and harness, wiping their cunts clean with a warm wet cloth so gently that Jerusha almost wept. "What about you?" he asked.

"You didn't hear me?" Magdalene said, humorously. "I had my pleasure three times, watching the two of you." She dropped the cloth into the basin and stripped off her clothing. "You'll stay the night, won't you?"

Lilias kissed Jerusha's cheek. "And tomorrow night, if you can. Will you stay with us, for a while?"

"I would," Jerusha said, "but I still must find work. I can't—I can't take your money, now, but..." He closed his eyes. "I don't know what to do."

Magdalene kissed him and climbed into the bed, snuggling him close between her and Lilias. "We'll speak of it tomorrow. I'm sure between the three of us, we can find a solution."

"You're not alone anymore," Lilias said, kissing him as well. "If you'll allow it."

Jerusha laid a hand atop each of them. "I will. Tomorrow," he said.

DYNAMIC DUO

J. Caladine

The online dating site sent me her profile as a match on the very first day. Her profile picture is a high-femme glam shot. I don't usually take that bait, but she looked like she was having a lot of fun, so I clicked. There were more pictures: gamine, shy, sexy librarian. That's bait I can't resist, so I read her profile. She said she was looking for people who are masculine-of-center and top-of-center: girls who are boys. Maybe that match system was onto something.

That's me right through. So I messaged her and invited her to check out my profile. What she found there was a picture of my best Italian, shiny, black, monk strap dress shoes, and the information that I am a confident butch top seeking femme play partners who need spanking. She wrote back, *This could work,* and asked for my picture.

I'm at a place in my life, my career and my geographic locale, where I can really be myself in terms of gender presentation. I'm thoroughly boyish. The only things in my wardrobe not from the men's department are the sports bras I use to flatten my chest. My hair is freshly clipped short on the sides and back every five weeks. I fuck with cock. But my dominant masculinity gains its fullest expression next to submissive femininity, which is what she brings. I'm taller, bigger and stronger, in a way that lets me envelop and contain her. My boxer briefs feel so much sexier in contrast to her little panties.

She's one of those few who can practically come with a sexy thought and a squeeze of her legs. She barely needs my help at all for that, so there is no resting on the laurels of physical technique. This one is all about the dynamic. She can tell me over email that she badly needs spanking and fucking and wants me to do it properly, but in person she is ever the ingénue. So my role is to manipulate, seduce and corrupt her into satisfying my wicked desires. In other words, I get to do almost anything I want, as long as I lead. Perfect.

When I know we're going to play, I think through each step of the scene for days beforehand. Tonight, I know what I'm going to do, and dress accordingly. Dr. Martens because I'm going to have her untie the laces. A nice belt because I'm going to have her unbuckle it. Harness on over boxers and under khakis so she'll see it when I make her unbutton my pants, and to save time, but no cock because she likes the one that's too big to pack. I choose a button-down dress shirt because I'll have her unbutton it.

She arrives wearing her coat over a dress and tights. She enters and awaits my instruction. I ask if she is ready. When she nods, I place my hand at the back of her neck and guide her into the next room (the one where we fuck) and direct her to place her hands on the wall. I press in close behind her with my mouth at her neck, and hear her breathing get shallower. I inhale her light scent: fresh-scrubbed innocence, laced with the faintest rebellion of cigarette smoke. After a few moments, I press forward just slightly against her ass and am rewarded with a gentle, involuntary return of pressure and a sharp intake of breath. She feels fantastic.

"Don't be scared, little one. I'll be nice if you behave. I'm always nice to the good girls." I pause to let that sink in, then continue: "Good girls do as they're told. They want to please. They have good manners, and pure thoughts."

"I'll be good, Sir," she says timidly.

"Good girls get gentle touches." I run my hands lightly up her sides and over her breasts and am again rewarded, this time with a small whimper of pleasure. "Bad girls are defiant. They are ill mannered and full of impure thoughts. Can you guess what bad girls get?"

"Spankings?" she asks, in a tiny voice.

"Exactly. Now, do you want to be a good girl for me?"

"Y-yes, Sir."

"Here's how: when I tell you to do something, you say 'yes, Sir,' and then you do it. Do you understand?"

"Yes, Sir."

"Okay, let's practice." I take a step away from the wall and stand in front of my armchair, then point to another chair across the room. I start with something easy. "Walk over there, take off your coat and put it on the chair. Then come back to me."

"Yes, Sir." She does it. I next have her kiss me on the cheek. This is also easy for my little innocent, but she forgets the honorific. I make her do it over, and then I reward her with gentle caresses, kisses and praise. Now it's time for the first challenge. I instruct her to walk back to the chair and take off her little cardigan sweater and dress and then return to me. She walks to the chair and removes her sweater but then just stands there. I guess that she wants help with her zipper (I'd failed to account for how ungraceful she might feel getting out of the dress herself) so I ask if she needs my help. She does. I walk over and unzip her dress, then retake my position across the room.

She slowly removes the dress and returns to me in just her tights and bra. I want her to feel exposed and a bit awkward, and she does. I put my hand on her shoulder and press down, ordering her to kneel. She does so, legs tightly together, big eyes gazing up at me. "Eyes down," I order. She just blinks at me.

This is actually a good sign. It seems less like she is balking at the command, and more like she didn't quite hear it, which means she is in the floaty subspace she craves. I repeat the command with a little more firmness and volume, and she quickly complies.

Next I tell her to untie my shoes. "Yes, Sir." When she has, I tell her she is a good girl, place my hand under her chin and lift her face toward mine. Our eyes meet, and I instruct her to get up and go back to the chair. Meanwhile, I remove my shoes. Once she's across the room, I tell her to remove her tights. This time she balks.

"That's not a request!" How I love an excuse to say that.

Still, she hesitates. "But, but, I'm not wearing anything under them, Sir," she whispers in protest.

"I don't care!"

Still she stands motionless. This is not acceptable. I close the distance in two strides, hook my thumbs into the waistband of her tights at each hip and strip them down to her ankles in one satisfyingly quick and fluid motion. She meekly lifts each foot in turn for me to remove her tights completely. I walk her back to my armchair and make her kneel again.

She kneels, her legs again pressed tightly together, eyes already down this time. I sit in my chair and lean forward so that my forehead presses on hers, my hand on the back of her neck. "I know you want to be a good girl."

"Yes, Sir, I do."

"You sound like a good girl. But I'm not sure." I slide my hand between her knees and give a gentle but firm push. She complies by opening her legs, feeling slightly nervous and unsure but excited about what may come next. I stroke her inner thigh and she lets out a little whine. I move my palm over her pussy and begin to stroke with my fingers, searching out her wetness. I am not disappointed, but do my best to sound so. "Ohhh, little one. When your pussy is wet, I know you've been having naughty thoughts."

"I'm, I'm sorry, Sir."

"I'll have to put you over my knee for this."

"Oh! No, Sir, please."

I grab her by the hair and pull her to her feet. She offers no resistance to this, nor to being placed across my knee. Heaven: her beautiful ass bare and ready for my attention. Her lovely face turned so I can see her eyes tightly shut in anticipation. I trap her legs between mine and began to caress her cheeks. But there won't be much warmup, as this is to be a brief, disciplinary spanking. A few smart slaps to each cheek and then some thuddy hitting between her legs with my closed fist. This always makes her come, and does now, though we both let this pass unremarked.

"Would you like another chance?"

"Yes, Sir."

I bring her back to the armchair and instruct her to unbutton my shirt. She gives a new sharp intake of breath as my shirt opens to reveal my female form under the masculine clothing. It is almost as if she is not quite expecting it, and is unable to fully conceal her delight. I hold her face in my hands and kiss her.

Then I make her kneel. Again she presses her legs tightly together. More kisses, then my forehead against hers and my hand between her thighs. Again, I push and she parts her legs. In the haze of subspace she has already forgotten what is about to happen. I stroke her pussy, which is even wetter after the spanking, and remark, "Still so naughty. You're a wicked girl."

Now she understands what's coming. "Ohhh," she moans in (mostly) mock dread, "I'm sorry, I'm sorry, Sir." Again, she offers no resistance as I put my fingers through her hair and persuade her to stand, but as I guide her into position she says, "Nonononono, please, I'll be good, I promise!"

"It's too late for that, little one." I spank her a little longer and harder this time, my own pussy beginning to pulse and swell with the sight and feel of her gorgeous, reddening ass. I finish with the thuddy hitting again, and then wait, with my palm against her skin, fingers spread wide to cover the entire small of her back until the spasms subside. I want my cock inside her.

Instead I bring her to her feet and back to the armchair. "Unbuckle my belt."

"Yes, Sir."

"And now my pants." She obeys, revealing the harness. "Bring me that." I point to a large, blue silicone cock (the one she picked when I gave her a choice) on the end table near the chair with her clothes. As she does so, I take off my pants and socks. When she returns with it, I have her kneel, eyes down, while I put it in my harness.

"Get on that couch!" I order, "With your ass up and your face down." She quickly does as she is told.

"Like this, Sir?" she asks.

"Yes, that's a good girl. Now you must show me that you really can be a good girl." As I lube my cock, I survey her, and my desire surges. Such a pretty little thing, and waiting so obediently for me to fuck her. I move forward and bring the tip of my cock flush with her wet opening. A few gentle thrusts and I'm halfway in.

She remembers her virtue and begins to protest. "No, no, I don't want it," she murmurs.

"You'll take whatever I give you, little one," I say sternly, and push the rest of the way in.

I hold her very firmly by the hips, and fuck her hard enough to make her drop character and start emitting "Yesyesyesyesyes" instead of "No." I love that. I bend forward, still inside her, and remove her bra and then my shirt. I let us both enjoy the feel of my bare stomach against her back, my hands on her breasts, and then I go back to hard fucking. I could continue like that for ages, but there are other things I want to do before our time is up.

I ease my cock out and guide her firmly to lie on her stomach. I remove my entire harness quickly, and put a finger cot over the index finger of my right hand. I lube it, put my knee between her open legs, spread her ass a little wider with my left hand and admire her. It's a stunningly attractive view. I begin to stroke her back door lightly with my fingertip. She's still kind of new to receiving attention there, and I know it instantly produces feelings of trepidation and submissiveness.

I cannot wait to feel that tightness from the inside, smoothness squeezing against me. My desire heightens again, the urge to fuck intensifying and my own wetness increasing. A gentle push is all it takes to slip all the way in. Her body can't pretend not to want it, and I know that shame and the exquisite physical sensation are working together to excite her intensely.

"Is it bad?" she asks tentatively. She wants my permission to enjoy it.

"Not if I want it."

"Okay," she says, so softly. "I don't want you to be angry."

"I'm not angry, little one. You're a very good girl to give me everything I want." I begin to push in earnest and, with my promised approval, she begins coming with equal fervor. Soon, my middle finger finds its way into her now-dripping pussy and both fingers work together to push her over a further edge. I feel them against each other through the thin wall that separates them, and then thrust inward. I love the undulating pressure: hard evidence of the pleasure I am giving.

It's another thing I could do for ages, but I know it's time to stop, so I slow, withdraw, toss the finger cot and take her into my arms. She releases a heavy sigh of satisfaction as she nuzzles into my shoulder and tucks her legs up against me, my arm over her thigh, hand on her ass. I adore that moment, but she soon has other ideas; other reasons she likes boys who are girls.

She knows, now, the way to get what she wants. She starts with light little kisses on my neck. Kryptonite. I'm nearly powerless to resist that sensation. She creeps up to my ear, but only for a moment, as kisses there make me wild to fuck instead of to receive. I remove my bra and boxer briefs and she lights up.

I let her explore as long as she is sweet and submissive about it. For a while I switch back every few minutes, my mouth on her nipples or fingers fucking her again, but soon I relent and let her stay inside me. My pussy constricts and ripples against her fingers and it's enough to set her off coming again. She's full of magic tricks like that. I'm still her opposite though. There's only going to be one orgasm, and we have to work together more than a few concentrated minutes to make it happen. That's just how it goes. But she's delighted to have me share it with her, which makes it unreservedly satisfying.

Too soon it's time for her to go. We both dress and share another moment of masculine presentation against feminine. There are a few more kisses and assurance offered in both directions that the scene went well. And then she's gone, until the next time.

LOBLOLLY

Tamsin Flowers

Wear something pretty," she said. "I'm taking you out."

I'm not great at doing pretty but when Jo asked for it, I wanted to do it right. I looked through my closet and picked a dress that used to be my sister's—spriggy blue flowers that would bring out the blue of my eyes and a crumpled lace trim that would lead her eyes to my cleavage. It was short but that was good—I knew already how much she liked my legs—and I matched it with an old pair of sneakers. I couldn't go too pretty, it just wouldn't be me.

Jo came to the house to pick me up like it was a proper date, which I suppose it was. By the time I answered the door, she'd stepped back and was lighting a cigarette on the bottom step of the porch. She looked good to me, in dark jeans, baggy enough to need the black braces which held them up and a wife-beater that showed off her tan skin and the sharp jut of her shoulders. She was skinny, boy skinny, but wiry with small, tight muscles that made me want to lick her. Underneath the white tank I could just see the dark circles of her nipples, protruding from the flat expanse of her chest, and the "Hello" I'd been about to say caught in my throat. Her bleached hair was cut short and shaved up the back, but the bangs at the front were long enough for her to hide behind when she wanted to.

She looked up at me and took a drag on her cigarette.

"Very cute," she said, exhaling a cloud of smoke. She dropped the cigarette on the path and ground it out with her heel. Then she stepped forward, took me by the wrist and kissed my cheek. "Come on."

The brush of her lips on my skin left a small imprint of heat, and the smell of her cigarette smoke up close turned me on to no end.

"You my girl?"

"Maybe," I said, skipping ahead of her on the path.

She drove a truck and I climbed up on the passenger side, feeling her eyes on the backs of my legs as I mounted the step. There were candy bar wrappers all over the seat and the ashtray was damn near overflowing with butts but the small space smelled of her. I don't have to tell you how much I liked that.

She got in and gunned the engine.

"Where're we going?" I said.

"Out to the forest," she said. "It's too nice to be indoors."

It was a beautiful day, though I'd hardly noticed it. The sun was sharp and Jo flipped down the sun visor against the glare.

"Should we stop and get wine?" I said.

"I got all we need, baby."

I studied her hands on the steering wheel. Small strong fingers with clipped white nails that stood out from her dark skin. Her grip was relaxed but I loved to watch the muscles and sinews of her arms moving under the surface as she turned corners and straightened up again. On her right bicep there was a tattoo of a pigeon. Not a dove or anything symbolic. Just a common wood pigeon, strutting across her arm, drawn in sharp, fine detail. I

don't know why she had it. On our second meeting I had asked
her about the fine white line that ran half an inch down her chin
from her lower lip.

"This scar," she said, fingering the mark, "is where this
bird"—she moved the tip of her finger to the tattoo—"flew into
me. Right into me, here, with its beak."

I laughed because I knew she was lying. If she had secrets she
wanted to keep that was fine with me. I had things of my own
that I wasn't going to spill anytime soon.

Several miles into the forest, a long way past the main
parking lot where families with dogs and children were
unloading, past the visitor center and nature trails, we came to
the end of the road. There was a turning circle and some gravel
standing for cars to park on but we were the only ones there.
Jo pulled a basket out of the back of the truck and we set off
into the trees.

Walking through dappled sun and shade, the only sound
the buzzing and chirruping of insects, I could almost hear my
heart humming. Jo was slightly ahead of me and I watched her
shoulder blades slip-sliding up and down under her skin as her
arms swung loose at her sides. I moistened my lips with my
tongue. She turned and caught me watching her.

"Let me take the basket for a while," she said.

We walked for half an hour and never saw another soul.
We were far deeper into the woods than the day-trippers went.
Jo was striding forward like she had a destination in mind but
I remembered she always walked fast in the city, head down,
cigarette in hand. I saw birds but I didn't know what sort they
were—I wasn't a nature lover and I only ever came out into the
forest when somebody else suggested it. But today it was nice,
walking through the trees with Jo in companionable silence.

Finally, she stopped and cast about herself some before dropping the basket down at the base of a tall, thin pine. She pulled

out a plaid blanket and spread it on the needle-strewn ground under the tree and invited me with a gesture to sit.

"This is a loblolly pine," she said.

"Is that rare?"

She laughed, the sun glinting on her white teeth, a string of saliva glistening between her dark lips. "Commonest tree in the forest, practically. But I just love it for its name."

I lay back on the blanket and looked up into the branches above me and at the small chinks of azure sky I could see through them. My heart was pounding hard and fast. I wanted her pretty bad.

"Loblolly," I said slowly, letting the word roll over my tongue. I closed my eyes.

A metallic jangle made me open them again just as Jo straddled my waist. Above me she was holding a pair of shiny steel handcuffs in one hand.

"You'll be okay with these," she said. It was more of a statement than a question and with her other hand she caught hold of one of my wrists.

My heart skipped a beat. No, make that several beats. I'd been hanging with Jo for maybe five or six weeks, having sex with her for the last two or three, but I had no idea she was into handcuffs. Or anything kinky like that. I'd never been handcuffed or tied up before.

"Jo?"

"Shhhh…" I felt the cold hard steel of the cuffs being pressed against my lips, crushing my unformed words of protest. I wriggled slightly but, although she wasn't any heavier than me, she had me pinned down.

"You need this, Ava," she said. "I could see it in you the moment I met you. You need someone strong to take you in hand."

She wasn't wrong about that, but she was the first one to try it this way. I looked to one side, at the trees stretching away as far as I could see, and I tried to calm my breathing. Then I nodded and held up my other wrist for her to take.

"Good girl," she said, her smoker's rasp always more in evidence when she was turned on. And I could tell by the brightness of her eyes and the flush of her cheek, she was turned on all right.

She put the cuffs on me and the metallic click of each bracelet closing sent a flash of longing up through my bowels. My mouth was dry and suddenly my whole body felt hypersensitive, as if every nerve ending had been uncovered. Stripped bare. I wanted Jo to touch me but I didn't know if I'd be able to bear it when she did. I think I gave a moan because she stroked my cheek and looked at me with such concern that I was suddenly frightened she would take the cuffs off.

"Wh-what are you going to do?" I said.

"First, I'm gonna make you secure."

She clambered off me and peered into the basket. A second later she hauled out a chain bicycle lock. She stretched it around the trunk of the loblolly tree behind my head and locked it. She leaned over me as she snapped the padlock shut, giving me a close-up view of her flat, taut abdomen at the top of her jeans. The skin there was not as brown as her hands and arms and I could see a fine smattering of downy blonde hair. Saliva flooded my mouth. Next she took a carabiner and used it to fasten my cuffed wrists to the chain. I could smell the sweat on her and I could see tiny droplets that had formed on the skin under her arms. I raised my head to see if I could lick them but she was moving and I wasn't quick enough.

Jo sat back on her heels and watched as I tested my restraints. She lit a cigarette and grinned at me.

"So pretty, Ava. You make me so happy."

I felt calmer and my breathing slowed as my heart rate started to approach normal.

"You trust me, don't you?" she said.

"Too late if I don't."

She carried on smoking on the edge of the blanket, savoring as she inhaled and holding the smoke in her lungs to get the best of the nicotine. When she exhaled I breathed in. I could almost taste her in the flavor of the tobacco. She ran two fingers slowly up the back of my calf, making my leg flinch.

"I think about you a lot when I'm not with you," she said. "Think about what I want to do to you. Think about what you need."

The surge of adrenaline her words precipitated made me shiver.

She stubbed out the cigarette and stashed the butt in a small metal tin she pulled from her jeans pocket. She tossed it into the basket when she finished. Then she turned back to me and lifted one of my feet into her kneeling lap. With her small, neat fingers, she undid the double knot I'd made in the laces and, placing one hand behind my heel, slipped off my sneaker. It was such a sensuous gesture, the way she did it, slow and smooth. I had a moment's panic about whether my foot smelled but then—shit—this wasn't about things like that. She raised my leg up and placed my foot against her shoulder. The flowery fabric of my dress slid down my thigh and pooled around my hips. The knowledge that she could see my panties made my cunt muscles clench. Oh, I was already wet.

She held the outside of my ankle and turned her head toward my leg. First her cheek pressed against the knot of my ankle joint, then I felt her tongue, warm and wet on my skin. I twitched but she held me firm, nuzzling my calf, while she let her other hand trail up to the back of my knee. I was breathing heavily and a hard ache of want was building up a head of pressure deep inside me.

"I always wanted a girl like you," she said, glancing up from my leg.

"Like me? How?" I said, my voice cracked with longing.

"You know, pretty but boyish at the same time. Who wore her need on her sleeve. Who was waiting for someone like me."

I swallowed.

"Who did you have a crush on when you were at school?" she said. "Not the jocks, was it?"

I shook my head.

"Or even the pretty girls, the popular ones? No, you liked the girls like me. I know that. That's why you're here in the woods with me, chained to a tree so I can do you whichever way I want."

She read me like a book and I loved it, even though I was nervous—no, scratch that—damned afraid of what she was going to do next. She took hold of my other foot and took off the sneaker in the same way but instead of placing my heel on her shoulder, she placed both my feet back on the ground, my knees still bent. I felt weak under her touch, like a rag doll, completely compliant. She dug into her pocket and drew out a penknife. Panic rose in my gullet. Was she really going to cut me?

"Don't," I whispered, almost choked with fear.

She stroked my thigh but didn't speak. Her touch didn't make me feel any calmer. I brought my knees together and pulled against the cuffs above my head. As she knelt up and loomed over me, the metal blade flashed in the sun. I thought I would faint. She reached forward and I twisted desperately. She placed a firm hand on my hip and held me still. There was a flash and a ripping sound at first one hip, then the other, and then I felt the back of my panties being pulled out from underneath me.

I could exhale. I could breathe again. Jo laughed and, tossing the knife aside, bent forward to kiss me. But I was cross now so instead of kissing her back, I bit her lower lip—hard enough to make her yelp, deep enough to draw blood. Only then did I kiss her back and was rewarded with her soft sigh of pleasure.

My sister's pretty dress was buttoned, so, when she'd finished kissing me, Jo undid the buttons one by one—and there were plenty—teasing my pale skin underneath with the fleeting touch of her fingers. Her blonde bangs hid her eyes but I could see her smile as I writhed under her hands. When they were all undone, she drew back the two sides of the dress like she was unwrapping a precious parcel and then, for a minute, she just looked at me, now virtually naked, apart from the dress pushed back at my shoulders, and completely ready for her.

My chest rose and fell with heavy breaths. She knelt between my legs and bent forward again. Her mouth alighted on my breast as softly as a butterfly but then she caught my other breast in her hand and pinched my nipple tight. The sharp pain was matched by her teeth nipping, and I bucked and kicked with my legs.

"You're like a new horse that needs breaking," she said, so I struggled some more to play up to the image. "And I will break you," she added.

Her words excited me. They made me want to fight against her, to see if she could really master me the way I wanted her to. She drew back, trailing kisses down my body, and planted her hands at the junctions of my thighs with my hips. She pressed my legs apart and I felt her warm breath on my labia. She breathed in deeply, smelling me, and exhaled across my clit. The warm air on my damp skin was enough to make me moan, and I let my hip joints soften so my legs could spread wider still.

I was already familiar with the feel of her small, pointed tongue tracing circles around my clit. But familiarity didn't breed contempt. It made me want it more. My hips flexed, pushing me up against her face until she was literally grinding her mouth and teeth into the soft crevices between my legs. Fingers pushed inside me, hard and harsh, just how I liked it. I could hear myself grunting and between the grunts, the sucking and slipping noises of a cunt being thoroughly worked over.

She could have let me come then and, although I was desperate for her to do just that, I would have been disappointed if things had been over that quickly. But Jo wasn't one for disappointment. And she wasn't one for a quick and easy screw. We hadn't walked all this way into the forest for a five-minute finger fuck. Even so, I felt bereft when her fingers pulled out of me and her mouth disengaged.

"Don't stop," I pleaded.

"I've got something better," she said, her voice as husky as ever.

She was kneeling over me again, still fully dressed. I squinted up at her—she looked so hot, I was trying to freeze the image onto my brain so I could hold on to the moment for as long as I needed it. She grinned and I smiled back. Her hand went to the zipper on her jeans and I heard the rasp as she pulled it down. She slipped her fingers inside, looking for all the world like a guy adjusting himself. Adrenaline and desire flooded me and my cunt clenched and pulsed till it hurt. When she'd finished rooting about inside her pants, the vision that emerged made me clench even more. It was sure going to hurt. My girl was brandishing a huge silicone cock, a beautiful, huge anatomical replica in inky black. It was way bigger than any flesh-and-blood cock I'd ever laid eyes on—not that that was saying much. I'd stopped sleeping with men pretty early on in my sexual career.

As soon as I saw it, I wanted it inside me. Deep inside me, moving in and out, hard and fast. But Jo was going to make me wait.

"You like?" she said, running her hand sensually along the never-ending shaft.

I nodded, panting too much to articulate the single word she wanted.

"Seriously, tell me you like it," she said.

"I like it." It didn't sound like my voice at all.

"And?"

"I want it."

"Where do you want it?" All the while she carried on stroking it and looking down at it, while I jerked at my cuffs, desperate to get to it.

"In my...cunt," I sobbed. "In my cunt." I spread my legs wide to show her I was ready.

She dove straight in, with a perfect aim at the perfect angle. I was so wet it just slid up through me like a hot knife through butter, stretching me with its enormous girth till it felt like I was burning. She immediately pulled back and plunged again, making me gasp, filling me up, and my muscles tightened around it all the more, so the next time she had to really pull to get it out.

As she fucked me and fucked me, I gazed up at her slack-mouthed face and her bright eyes. At the cords of sinew standing out along her neck and the hard tension in the muscles of her shoulders and upper arms. At her blonde hair, now damp and floppy with sweat, and the dark, wet patches forming on her wife-beater. It flapped forward every time she came forward, giving me a glimpse of her small, pointed nipples.

We were both panting and moaning but as she pushed me over the edge, as my orgasm took hold, I screamed. Deep in the forest I screamed and screamed, raising a flurry of wood pigeons, flapping and squawking, out of the bushes. And without letting up her rhythm, she pushed one hand down between us and grasped my clit, pulling on it hard, yanking and twisting until I came some more and screamed even louder.

Finally she pulled out. She knelt above me, her black cock dripping and shining with my juices. She thrust a hand down the waist of her jeans, behind the dildo, and rubbed. With her other hand she grabbed one of her nipples underneath the tank and twisted. Her back arched and she grunted low in her throat, muscles juddering. Then she flopped down on the blanket beside me, the wet dildo smacking my thigh hard enough to raise a bruise.

I turned my head and bit her shoulder, sucking at the same time, to leave a mark.

She smiled at me and undid the handcuffs, kissing each wrist as she released it.

"You're my girl now," she said.

FIVE BLOW JOBS

Sinclair Sexsmith

I

After the workshop, I still haven't had enough of you (will I ever get enough of you?) and strip you bare, glove my hand, slide two fingers inside you, sideways on our huge king bed. The lamplight is different than the bright white of this room during the day, more warm, orange-yellow-gold and more full of shadows, and the shadows and the gold fall onto your skin like paint.

In the car on the way back I couldn't resist (can rarely resist, it's so hard to resist when part of our dynamic is built around taking what I want) and slid your small fingers into my mouth. You missed the exit.

Your fingers are blunt and I trace your jagged nails with my tongue, suck the salt from the pads, taste the day on your skin. I pull your wrist down to your pelvis and take two fingers in my mouth again when my two fingers are inside you, gently pressing, not a lot of motion, and I start to suck you off. Up and down your fingers like a cock. I hold your G-spot and feel it quiver in my fingers. I let your fingers out of my mouth so you can touch your clit, and keep my tongue on the back of your hand. You shudder and convulse against my mouth, your cunt grips my fingers. You slide your fingers back in my mouth, eager, and I taste you, just a little, at the tips, and I do it all over again.

II

On the side of the bed, but you're not supposed to be coming that day, and you do. It sneaks up on you in a moan, but before you can really come you stop yourself, blurting out, "Fuck!" again, and it's the second time you've come without permission, and you're in trouble. You back off and look at me shyly; I am laughing at your distress, you just feel so bad for defying the rules, and the guilt is more than enough punishment. I can feel how badly you want to please me. I am enjoying this too, too much: your attempts to do things just right and your scrambles to fix it when you are so happy, so pleased to be serving me, servicing me, kneeling before me, my cock in your throat. It's enough for you to see that look on my face, that ecstasy you're causing, that overwhelming lust and adoration as your tongue hits the head so soft and slow as you suck it down, which makes me want to pulse and shoot, makes me feel my balls (as if I had them) contract and swell, cocked and loaded. You move back toward my dick with your lips parted and I push you away. "No—I think you're done sucking my cock. You lost that privilege when you came without asking. Down. Kiss my boots."

III

Long, slow aftercare. I let the beating settle into your body—the belt, my hands, the restraints on your ankles and wrists. After some time on the bed I move us to the chair so you can sit on my lap. You wrap around me, sink down. You quiet and calm and I ask, "Ready to suck my cock again?" You say yes, quickly,

in a whisper, and kneel between my knees. I loosen the harness
and touch my clit under it while you suck me down. (You're not
supposed to come today, still; one of us may as well.) "Good
boy," I breathe as I watch your mouth, tongue, lips, my cock
down your throat. I let you guide it. I let you slide it however
deep you want. I push a little, because that's what I do, but
mostly I just concentrate on the feeling and the sight. I almost
come but it's too much, I get overstimulated and don't have the
right angle so I get up and take my jeans off, my socks and shoes
and briefs, and spread my legs wider, get a better grip under
the harness. You start in again and I imagine what your mouth
would feel like. I know every inch of it, know every ridge of the
roof and every taste bud on your tongue and every valley of your
teeth with my fingers and my tongue, but fuck how I wish I could
feel those with my cock. We are making do with what we have
and you are an expert at sucking me down, swallowing, and I
think about how I'd get tight and build up pressure, ready to
shoot. You moan around my cock and I feel it in my pelvis and
I feel you squirt on my ankle and foot; you're straddling my leg.
"Ohh fuck you're in trouble," I manage. You whimper a little,
give me those eyes, those sweet little boy eyes like you would do
anything for your Daddy, you're sorry, you didn't mean to, you
couldn't help it, and it doesn't take long before I'm over the edge
for you, coming in your mouth, yelling out and curling my spine
and feeling how I'd shove and come to the back of your throat. I
breathe, my body stills. You sink down onto your belly and put
your tongue to my foot, clean it off, suck my instep. With your
head still down low, you say, "Am I still in trouble?" and I laugh.

IV
You walk over to me with your cock on, hard and thick and
fitting you, jutting out from your hips. "Can you stand?" I ask.
You nod. I sit on the edge of the bed. You let me feel it, with

my hands and along my lips, my jaw, getting to know its new contours. I put my tongue on it, kiss it, and you shudder. I like feeling how hard you are in my mouth. I can't take it as deep as I think I can, but I try, again and again, wanting you so far inside.

V

You start on your knees at the end of the bed after I have kicked you, hit you with my belt, after I told you to pick a number and you picked three, after you took more than you thought you could, after you crawled for me, after my hands in you at the edge when I said come on and shoot that load for your Daddy, little faggot, and I shove in, impatient and hard, to the back of your throat. You gag. I keep going. I hold you by the hair and work my hips so it goes in and out of your mouth. You gag again. I keep going. I stand over you and you rise up a little higher and I keep fucking your mouth. I wrap my hand around your throat. I pinch your nose closed and shove in. You look up at me, pleading, in a rare moment of eye contact. I don't let up until I count to ten. I take my dick out and let you breathe and do it again. Count to ten. Sometimes I hold my breath with you, but I always let mine go before you do. I fist your hair and shove in deep. My hips shake against your mouth. Come on, little boy, take it, that's right, that's how I like it, fuck, yeah, give me that pretty little mouth, take it deeper, you can do better than that, fucker, do it, suck it down, yeah that's right, nice. You stumble back a little and my fist holds you up.

Always.

NOT JUST HAIR

Annabeth Leong

Darla thought she knew all the butches in town, but even in the dim lighting of the play party, she was sure she'd never met this one. From behind, the woman looked deliciously strong—far too muscular to be described as slight despite her compact build.

The sight of her made Darla lick her lips. Just her type. She hoped this time she'd found someone who wanted to play her way, too.

Darla clutched her rope bag. It had been a big step for her to buy it since the vast majority of her kink experience had been as a bottom. She still wasn't sure she could live up to the expertise that the black bag seemed to promise. A few attempted scenes using borrowed rope, however, and she'd learned how hard it was to be taken seriously when she was using another top's toys. It was hard enough to be a girly girl looking for tough leather-clad types who wanted to play the sub role, and harder still when all the locals had seen Darla suspended and squealing with delight too many times to treat her as a dominant. She didn't need to add any handicaps she didn't already have.

The nice thing about meeting a stranger such as the sexy butch across the way was that it gave Darla a chance to start fresh. In this moment, before they had spoken, Darla could fantasize that this was the woman she'd been looking for—the butch who didn't see bottoming as a threat to her masculinity, the lover who would be as thrilled by experimentation as Darla was.

Taking a deep breath, Darla edged closer. The newcomer had dyed her buzz cut a brilliant, defiant pink that showed up nicely amid the otherwise muted colors in the room. That seemed like a good sign, a declaration of some sort of in-between space where Darla might fit.

No longer seeing the shadowy couples around her with their rope and paddles, Darla made for that breath of butch fresh air, the party's sinuous music informing the movements of her hips. She'd oiled her leather miniskirt until it was supple enough that it didn't creak as she moved, it sighed.

Once she got close enough to catch her quarry's scent, she liked that, too. Her cologne smelled clean and woodsy, a light fragrance with a hint of animal energy underneath. Darla had forgotten the rest of the party the moment she laid eyes on the unfamiliar guest, so it was a bit of a surprise to find herself at the edge of a small crowd that had gathered around a spanking scene.

She knew the players—a showy femme popular for the ease with which her pale asscheeks turned cherry red and a fierce top who could swing away all night and never get tired. Fun stuff for anyone who hadn't seen it a hundred times before.

The newcomer seemed supremely nervous watching it, though, scratching at the short, bright hairs at the nape of her neck every few seconds and tugging at her leather vest as if it itched. She didn't carry a toy bag, and Darla wondered if she'd stashed it somewhere, had come only to watch or, wonder of wonders, had shown up hoping to bottom.

Darla had to know. She formed a rapid plan, her face and hands feeling a little hot. She wasn't used to being this aggressive, but she didn't often get the chance to be. She could welcome this woman to town, then work her way into a discussion of what they each hoped to get out of the play party, and maybe by then she'd know if she had a shot at doing a scene.

With a few determined steps, she closed the rest of the distance between them and placed herself at the other woman's left shoulder. "I haven't seen you here before," she said, pitching her voice to a low purr. "I thought I'd take the chance to welcome you before some other femme snaps you up."

She glanced up with a practiced flirtatious motion, first looking through her eyelashes, then snapping her lids open to reveal the stunning violet shade of the colored contacts she wore. The effect could be magnificent when Darla didn't end the process with her jaw dropped open, gaping. "Shawna?"

The woman she'd been watching wasn't a stranger. Darla and Shawna had come to these play parties together countless times, with and without their girlfriends. Just two months ago, Shawna's longtime girlfriend, Andi, had tied their hands together, palm to palm, and led them to a spanking bench. She'd helped Shawna lie on her stomach on the bench, still connected to Darla, who wound up kneeling by her head. Then Andi spanked Shawna until she cried and gripped Darla's hands so hard it hurt, while Darla's top made her lick the tears away. At some point during the scene, Darla and Shawna had kissed. Nothing had been real for Darla after that except for the heat of Shawna's tongue, the occasional scrape of her teeth and the silk of her soft, plump lips, which were slightly sticky from the remnants of her sweet-smelling strawberry lip gloss.

That kiss had bothered Darla for weeks because she wasn't used to being attracted to women like Shawna—at least, not women who looked the way Shawna had every other time that

Darla had seen her. Always dressed to the highest height of femme, Shawna had eyebrows drawn on, eyes shaded with a masterful blend of brown and gold tones, nails painted a shimmering pink and long blonde hair smoothed into the soft waves of a 1940s movie star. Everything about her had looked, smelled and tasted of cream and sugar, and that wasn't anything Darla had ever thought she wanted.

As certain as Darla was that this was in fact Shawna, the same body and the same face, almost nothing about her seemed the same. Aside from the haircut and dye job, she'd let her eyebrows grow in thick. Unadorned by makeup, the lines of her face had taken on a stubborn handsomeness that made Darla wonder how she had ever seemed so delicate and sweet. And those muscles—had Shawna always been so strong, so immaculately gym sculpted?

The fine specimen of butch in front of her was making Darla juice up and swoon, but also question reality. She stammered as she stared, but couldn't form a complete question.

Shawna flushed, and the pink that came to her cheeks reminded Darla even more of the way she used to look. "I'm trying out Shawn these days," she told Darla.

The difference wasn't only in her look—she treated Darla differently, too. A slight teasing quality crept into Shawn's voice, and her jaw tightened as she took in Darla's curves with blatant flicks of her gaze. Her dark eyes hardened with approval, instead of softening. This new version of Darla's old acquaintance knew how to praise femininity with a series of shifts of her demeanor, and she made Darla ache to respond, to apply every soft line of herself as contrast, to make Shawn feel big and firm all over.

If this had been a stranger, Darla would have begged to start a scene then and there, giving in at once to the powerful, primitive reactions swirling through her body. However, since this was a dramatically different version of a woman she'd thought she'd known, words seemed necessary. A few of them, at least.

"Where's Andi?" Darla asked, remembering Shawn's stern, inventive girlfriend.

"We broke up."

"You cut your hair."

"You noticed." Shawn delivered the reply in a dry tone that also didn't fit with the bubbly persona that Darla had always associated with her.

Darla sensed that it would be best to respond in kind. "It's a subtle change, but I pride myself on my powers of observation."

Shawn grinned at that, and the effect made Darla gooey again. That wide, boyish smile—why had she never perceived it the way she did now? "Thanks for that. You're the first person who hasn't scolded me about making such a drastic change so soon after a breakup." She shrugged defensively. "It's just hair."

As a self-respecting femme, Darla couldn't let the comment pass. "It's not just hair, and you know it. I'm not going to judge you, but don't lie."

Shawn opened her mouth to respond, but the spanking going on nearby intruded with a set of sharp, staccato slaps in quick succession and the accompanying shrieks. Feeling bold, Darla grabbed Shawn's hand. "Let's find a spot of our own." The newly minted butch gave no resistance to the tug. Excitement built in Darla's chest, making her feel as if her ribs would need to stretch to contain it all. She kept thinking about that scene they'd shared, and that kiss, and wondering if Shawn's transformation explained the chemistry Darla had felt.

Darla staked out a free corner for them, set down her rope bag, and steered Shawn into a sitting position on an unused bondage table.

"It wasn't a whim," Shawn said immediately, obviously needing to get the statement off her chest. "I've been thinking about doing this for years, it's just that it upset Andi so much every time I brought it up. It threatened her masculinity to picture me doing it, I think."

Darla couldn't help raising an eyebrow at that. "You've been the girliest of the girly girls for years, but the whole time you were wishing you could cut your hair short and switch to pants?"

"A lot of that time. Yes."

Darla blinked a few times. Shawn and Andi had been together for what seemed like forever, and she tried to imagine how stifling that must have felt. She could understand the skepticism Shawn faced, too, at least on some level. She'd had versions of this conversation herself when she'd tried to explain that she didn't want to bottom anymore. She'd been brought into the scene as a bottom, and by the time she figured out the lay of the land enough to think she might want to top, she'd been entrenched in a relationship and the roles that came with it.

And she knew how touchy people could be about shifting roles. Years ago, Darla had naively believed that coming out as a lesbian would put an end to agonizing conversations about her sexual identity, but in fact those moments had marked a beginning. Ever since, it seemed she'd been struggling to figure out and articulate more about what she wanted to do and how she wanted to do it, and to negotiate with partners about whether what she wanted was okay.

Shawn cleared her throat, obviously still concerned about Darla's reaction to her recent shift. "People keep telling me I should have started smaller, that cutting off my hair is too drastic, but I didn't want to creep up on it. I wanted to do it. I've been craving the freedom."

Darla had no trouble understanding this. "Some changes can't be made halfway."

Shawn met this with a vigorous nod. "Exactly."

The moment stretched, and Darla became painfully aware

that she'd placed Shawn on a bondage table. Her body had never stopped reacting to Shawn as a sexy butch. She had to know a little more. Darla bit her lip. "How about your kink role?" she asked.

Shawn's face fell. "I can't tie you up, baby. I don't think I'm a top." She sighed. "It would be so much easier if I were, but I don't think I want to switch."

Unconsciously, Darla began to bounce on the balls of her feet, lifting her stiletto heels off the ground. Before she considered her actions, she leaned in and brushed her mouth against Shawn's.

The slightly chapped lips she encountered surprised her, but the jolt she felt didn't. It was hard to imagine anyone more attractive than Shawn at this very moment, full of pent-up masculine energy she'd been dying to express, hard lines and raw possibilities.

Shawn touched her fingers to her face after Darla pulled away. "What was that for?"

"I want you."

Her eyebrow climbed. "Really?"

Darla unzipped her rope bag. "Hell, yeah. My ex-girlfriend didn't like the idea of bottoming for me because it threatened her masculinity. I've got a feeling that's not going to bother you." She pulled out a coiled length of hemp and unfurled it with a practiced flick of her wrist. "Do you want to play?"

Shawn didn't challenge Darla's switch at all, instead licking her lips as her eyes followed the motions of Darla's hands.

A sense of beauty and power filled Darla, making her notice the way her manicured red nails slid between the strands that made up the hemp, the way her white jasmine perfume contrasted with the rope's aura of hard, heavy work. Shawn's eyes were what made her see herself this way, the lustful awe in them reflecting the image that Darla most wanted to embody.

Exhilaration quickened her pulse. This was the way that only a hot butch could make her feel—seen, recognized, opposed in the sexiest way.

She tried to give it all back to Shawn, to show her how the sight of her tight, muscular strength from across the room had made her want to trap that energy for her own pleasure. Darla tossed one end of the rope onto the table beside Shawn and cocked her head to one side.

"If I agree to bottom, does that make you think I'm still a femme deep down? Because that's what some people have said." Shawn laughed a little. "I guess maybe it does threaten my masculinity."

Darla clambered onto the table beside her. She wanted to start tying so badly her fingers itched. "Are you going to feel like a femme deep down after I tie you up and get lipstick prints all over every one of these sexy muscles of yours?" Darla touched the tip of her fingernail to the firm flesh of Shawn's upper arm and pushed just hard enough to give the gesture a little sting. "Are you going to feel like a femme deep down after I make sure you can't move at all and then rub my pussy up and down your thigh until my lacy panties can't stop you from feeling how wet I am for your cock?" She dipped her head toward Shawn's ear, making sure her dark, silky hair brushed the butch's cheek. "How about after I make you tell me how hard you are for me, over and over, then spank you for all the naughty things you admit you want to do?"

"Jesus." Shawn gripped Darla's arms, squeezing tightly enough to show off the strength in her hands. "You know how to make me want you, baby."

Darla pulled back so their eyes could meet. Shawn's eyes flashed with satisfaction that Darla recognized. They had entered each other's worlds. Between them, there could be no more questions. Darla accepted Shawn's vision of herself, and vice versa. She reached for the rope. "Play with me? Please?"

"God, yes."

"Good," Darla purred. She had practiced so much at home, afraid of embarrassing herself if she did manage to find a butch who would bottom for her, that it was second nature to flip Shawn onto her stomach and secure her hands behind her back. The other woman twisted her head to watch Darla straddle her ass, her eyes wide.

Darla picked up on her nervousness and stroked the side of Shawn's face. "It's all the same," she said. "You know the drill, the party safewords. You know me."

"Nothing is the same at all."

Darla's lips curved. Shawn had a point. She emphasized it by yanking her black shirt over her head, revealing the red leather bra underneath. It wasn't only Shawn who had changed. She felt stronger, too, more centered in her identity as a femme top than she had ever been when she'd tried to play the polite submissive.

"Maybe it's not the same," Darla said. "You used to be such a good girl for Andi, but that wasn't the real you, was it?"

Shawn shook her head.

"So what is the real you? Do you just let a woman tie you up? Or do you flex those muscles and put up a fight?"

"You have no idea how much I want to fuck you right now, Darla."

Darla reached behind herself and administered a quick, hard smack to the back of Shawn's thigh, grinning at the way it startled the woman beneath her. "What the hell?" Shawn said.

"You're being a naughty butch. That's why I have to tie you up. I have to protect myself from your dangerous desires."

"My dangerous desires? You have no idea."

"Oh, I think I do." Darla supported herself by placing one hand on Shawn's shoulder and maneuvered herself off the table so she could stand beside Shawn. With quick, decisive twists and tucks, she secured Shawn's ankles to each other with a double-column tie, then bent down to whisper in her play partner's ear again. "I wouldn't be safe if you were free."

Shawn was starting to get into the way Darla was playing. The muscles in one arm twitched, and a second later she began to wriggle and struggle on the table. "You're not keeping that sweet little pussy away from me. I'm going to take it."

If Darla hadn't needed to keep the scene going, she could have just stood back and watched those muscles rippling. Her cunt pulsed. She'd wanted it just like this for so long—had wanted to feel the rush of having a powerful, unbreakable butch under her control.

She wanted to put a chest harness on Shawn, too, to give herself a handle to use to haul her butch around, and to watch the rope shift in time to the heaving of her lungs. Darla briefly berated herself for tying Shawn's hands before wrapping rope around her chest, knowing that would complicate matters. On the other hand, she knew she had to cut herself some slack for her first real scene as a top. She couldn't expect to do everything perfectly her first time out, and what really mattered was keeping the scene hot for both of them.

She placed a hand on the back of Shawn's neck, gripping there as if she were handling a baby lion. "I need you to flip over for me," Darla said. "I'm going to show you how to do some nice cuddling."

"I don't want to cuddle," Shawn snarled. "I want to tear that bra off with my teeth."

Darla grinned. She wanted that, too, but it was so much fun to pretend she didn't. She made a clucking noise with her tongue. "See, this is why I need to get more rope on you. Flip over."

Shawn growled, but rolled onto her back. Darla touched the side of her arm, marveling at the way the tie held her taut, her muscles half-flexed. She picked out a new length of rope and helped Shawn sit up, her legs stretched out in front of her, the ankles pulled together. "I'll bet you want to see my nipples," Darla said.

"Oh god."

"Yeah, I thought so. If you behave yourself and let me put a harness on you, I'll let you see them. If you're really good, I might let you suck them. What do you think?"

"I think this had better not be a trick."

"Oh, it's not a trick at all," Darla said coyly. "I want you to see my nipples, I just have to make sure I'm safe when I show them to you."

"I'm going to suck them until you forget all about the ropes. Then I'm going to break free and show you how hard you've been getting me." The fire in Shawn's voice took Darla's breath away. She loved seeing Shawn crazy to get loose from the ropes and fuck her.

She bit the top of Shawn's ear as she fumbled with the beginning of the harness, using her teeth to warn the other woman to hold still. Darla built up rope around Shawn's chest, threading it under her arms, thrilled by every incidental touch that happened in the process.

When Darla was tied up, meditative peace usually settled over her. That wasn't happening now at all. With every additional bit of rope she added, the tension between the two of them tautened. Sexual energy vibrated in every shift of the rope, transferring from her body to Shawn's and back again.

"Where are those nipples?" Shawn growled.

Darla tightened the grip of her teeth to remind them both who was in charge, then ran some rope through the harness and attached it to a ring at the head of the table. Leashed to the table, hands tied behind her back, ankles hobbled, Shawn wouldn't be able to do much that Darla didn't allow. None of these ties made her seem weak, though. Like a big cat in a cage, Shawn exuded a sense of prowling menace that thrilled Darla to the core. She wanted to play with her restrained butch, dizzy from desire and the risk of approaching Shawn's ever more obvious lust.

Darla stepped away from the table, out of Shawn's range. There, she reached behind her back and unsnapped her bra, easing the cups down to reveal her tightened nipples. "You want to lick these, right?" Head pounding from the rush of exposing herself to Shawn's appreciative gaze, Darla let the bra fall, then ran her hands down her sides, squeezing the soft flesh of her belly and toying with the zipper that would release her miniskirt.

"That's it, baby," Shawn said. "You bring that over here for me."

"You want to feel how wet my pussy is, don't you?"

"Quit teasing and I'll show you."

"I'm not teasing," Darla protested innocently. "I'm being careful." She freed herself from the miniskirt and slowly came toward where Shawn sat. Keeping a wary eye on the ties, Darla straddled Shawn's legs and inched her chest toward Shawn's mouth.

"I'm going to make those nipples feel so good," Shawn crooned. "Just a little closer."

Darla grinned, moving to the very edge of where she thought Shawn could reach. Shawn stretched her tongue forward, the tip of it forming a trembling point as she strained to reach Darla's left nipple.

Giving in slightly, anxious to feel that touch, Darla closed the gap between her chest and Shawn's mouth, groaning at the rough wetness of Shawn's first lick. The pressure that had been building since Darla laid eyes on Shawn erupted at this contact. Darla needed to release it, and she reached around Shawn's body to the back of her harness and tugged her backward until she came off the nipple, leaving her mouth free for Darla's kiss.

Darla wanted to eat Shawn, to put a mark on her. This time, she didn't content herself with a subtle touch of lip to lip. She pulled at the harness with both hands to make Shawn feel how she'd trapped her, and staked her claim with a hungry, wide-open mouth. Shawn growled into the kiss and brought her thighs up, pushing hard against Darla's ass. The force made Darla slip out of position and fall directly onto Shawn's crotch, her pussy pressed against the bulge that Shawn had packed into her tight leather pants.

"Mmmm." Shawn broke free of the kiss, and the hard strength in her eyes made Darla feel as if she dangled on the edge of something far bigger than she could handle. "Do you like that? You want to feel how hard I am for you?" She bucked her hips, managing to shift them both despite her restraints.

Darla shrieked and clung to the harness for balance, her head spinning.

"Give me those nipples," Shawn said. "You promised."

Darla nearly obeyed, the submissive in her well-trained. Then she remembered her new role and dipped her head beside Shawn's for a moment, desperate to control her breathing and regain her ability to think straight. "You're so dangerous," she whispered in Shawn's ear. "I think I need to use more rope."

Shawn cursed. "I need to fuck you." She nipped at Darla's throat, and Darla wanted her so badly that she very nearly abandoned her role as top. Her pussy tingled against Shawn's leather-covered crotch.

She pulled herself away before Shawn could tempt her to give in completely. "Those naughty teeth!" Darla said. "We're going to have to see what else we can do here."

She jumped away from her play partner again and attached a line to Shawn's ankles, then anchored that beneath the table. Tugging gently, Darla pulled Shawn's legs down the surface until she lay straight and flat, stretched between the rope connected to her harness and the new attachment that Darla had just made. "Are your hands okay tied behind your back?" she asked. "Not too much pressure on your wrists?"

"You know where the pressure is," Shawn said.

"Yeah, I do." Darla formed her best wicked smile and tapped a finger against her clit. "Now that I'm sure you'll behave, I'm ready to take care of it."

Once more, she climbed onto Shawn, who struggled beneath her. "Take out my dick," she ordered, but Darla grinned and ignored the request.

"Such a strong, sexy butch," Darla said, running a finger along Shawn's pulsing biceps. "Let's see how wet I've gotten." She rubbed her panty-covered crotch along Shawn's thigh, squeezing her legs around the hard, straining muscle she found there. A few more firm passes, and her panties slipped to one side, placing Darla's clit and labia in direct contact with Shawn's leather pants. The trail of arousal she left down the front of Shawn's thigh glistened in the dim light of the party. "Ooh," Darla said, running a finger through it. "See what I've got?"

She waved her cunt-scented fingertip under Shawn's nose, but deftly avoided her partner's efforts to suck it.

"I don't trust those naughty teeth of yours," Darla said.

"Baby, you're killing me. I need your pussy."

"Oh, don't worry. I'm going to put it right on your dick." Darla maneuvered her crotch onto Shawn's bulge and rocked until she found the best spot to settle. "See? You've got it. I'm just going to make myself come with this hard, hot body of yours."

She began to move, savoring the feeling of Shawn straining but constrained between her thighs. The scene had worked Darla up so much that she could have come the moment she began to rub against Shawn's package, but she forced herself to slow down. Making eye contact with Shawn, she began to rub and tweak her nipples while ostentatiously pleasing herself.

"You are going to let me fuck you," Shawn panted, but she sounded close to orgasm herself by now. Darla grinned and circled her hips, noticing how her grinding seemed to hit the spot for Shawn as well.

Shawn joined the rhythm despite remaining encased in leather and rope. Darla teased a little more. "I'll do what I want," she said. "I know how big and tough you normally are, but I've got you all tied up now, so I'll be the one calling the shots."

Groaning, Shawn let out a string of curses, all while rocking her hips so hard she nearly unseated Darla. "I'll get free when your back is turned, and then you won't be able to play cute with me anymore. I'll show you what I've got for you, baby, and you're going to love it."

Shawn's threats were too much for Darla. Throwing her head back, she let the orgasm come. Shawn continued to grind through her spasms, never letting her forget the heat of the woman beneath her. When Darla could, she brought her gaze back to Shawn's face.

The other woman had squeezed her eyes closed, and a fine layer of sweat made her skin shine. She grunted and panted with the effort of fighting the ropes and Darla's weight, and she looked magnificent. Feeling renewed awe at Shawn's transformation from high femme to powerful butch, Darla watched her claw her way to orgasm.

Darla leaned forward and grabbed Shawn's earlobe, pinching, reminding her of the control she'd been exerting. With that harsh guidance, she led her partner the last bit of the way. Shawn gritted her teeth and growled as her climax struck, pressing her crotch up toward Darla's pussy in a trembling frenzy.

Watching Shawn lose focus and then reform herself, slowly restoring the arrangement of muscles that had gone wayward in search of pleasure, Darla wondered about the images that had ruled for so long in both their sex lives. Were these newest selves also their truest selves?

Shawn blinked up at Darla, an old, sweet vulnerability in her dark eyes now. "Damn, baby, that was hot. We've got to do more."

The warmth that spread through Darla's chest as they smiled at each other laid her questions to rest. She wasn't afraid to change if she had to—she'd been through so many transformations that had cost her, and come out in this moment, alive and satisfied. Shawn, too, could face and survive a metamorphosis. She touched her fingers to Shawn's lips and hoped they could find a way to keep changing together.

WHAT I'M MADE OF

Kyle Jones

We worked at a sandwich shop together. I was eighteen and fresh out of high school; she was a little older. From day one, I was completely infatuated with her and she knew it, teasing and tormenting me through every shift. She flirted in a way that left wet spots in my khakis. She was that good."

I had been talking to a friend about past loves and it wasn't until near the end of the conversation that this one ex-lover in particular had come to mind. I'd put a lid over those memories for a long time, sealing off the pain and confusion I'd associated with her. As I unpacked that period of my life, what I found was not the bitter pain I'd been guarding against, but memories sweetened by time, a story I could finally savor and share.

The first time I saw her, during the orientation tour behind the counter, she was facing away, adding ice to the salad bar. I was supposed to be following the manager, but instead I followed her curves with my eyes. She turned around, caught me looking and winked. *Oh crap,* I thought, *I'm in trouble.* It was a very knowing wink, one that stopped me dead in my tracks and made me blush for the first of a million times. Meanwhile, the manager was going on about the equipment and supplies and my responsibilities. It took a lot of effort to wrench my attention back to the seven varieties of bread, which I needed to memorize before the start of my second shift. Once he'd finished showing me around, he introduced me to her and told me to follow her lead—she'd teach me everything I needed to know.

I didn't have a clue how prophetic that statement would ultimately be. She took me under her wing as a sandwich maker, showing me the ropes and instructing me in the specific quirks of our many regulars. This instruction was liberally spiced with double entendres and not-so-accidental touches that made me squirm and blush. It wasn't long before she had me completely wrapped around her little finger.

I was always eager to please, jumping at any chance to impress her, willing to do anything so she'd smile at me or say something flirty and appreciative. She wasn't twenty-one yet, but she had friends who were and sometimes, when we were closing together, she'd pull out a couple of beers to share. I'd get all fuzzy headed and goofy and she'd sit on my lap and tease the short hairs at the back of my neck and call me her "cute little butchy butch." I was such a goner. If anybody else had called me that, I'd have given him or her a look from hell, but she could say anything and I'd always react as if she'd given me the highest compliment.

I remember hearing about boyfriends, or "boy friends" (she always corrected me). She didn't seem serious about any of them, and there was a new one every couple of weeks. She'd occasionally hint about having past experience with girls, too, and would encourage me to tell her about my ex-girlfriends. My stories, very bland in comparison to hers, were a source of great amusement for her, if her laughter was any indication.

One night, after regaling me with stories of her latest fling and how she'd kicked him to the curb, she grabbed me by the belt buckle and pushed me up against the door of the walk-in freezer.

"So...you have plans tonight, Butch?" She said "Butch" in a sweet, sexy purr that made my heart thump wildly and my face blush neon red. When she put her hand on my cheek, my knees almost buckled. It was a moment I'd fantasized about and I'd always imagined being so smooth, but instead my words stumbled out, "Oh, uh-um, nothin' much, I don't think, uh, how about you?"

Her eyes narrowed to a predator's gaze. "Nothing much, huh? Well then, we should do something. Together." The last word was less like a suggestion than an order. Or a threat. "Let's close up early."

She didn't wait for an answer, or, more likely, she took my dumbstruck look as "Yes," and began going through the closing procedures. I stood in shock for a second or two, considering the implications of what I'd just heard and hoping I wasn't mistaken. Was she inviting me on a date? Was I gonna get some tonight? With her! She caught my eye and raised an eyebrow. I shook off my shock and began wiping tables and emptying trash cans before she could change her mind.

Twenty minutes later, she pulled the car into a spot overlooking the lake. I had a feeling she'd known the light was out at this end of the parking lot. She leaned back and sighed, looking across the lake, where the moonlight was pooling. I stared at her breasts, mesmerized by the way they moved under her thin tank top, captivated by the exposed skin of her shoulders and collarbones. She turned back to me and took my hand, placing it on one breast. I exhaled with a groan, expressing the pent-up desire I'd been stifling for months. She chuckled, low and dark, looking at me from under her eyelashes. I squeezed her lightly, still unsure that this was actually happening and not just an elaborate tease. She pressed against my hand and smiled wickedly.

Her fingers stroked my cheek, then trailed down my neck and across my chest, her palm coming to rest like a warm ember over my heart. I sighed deeply, relaxing into her touch, eyes half-shut. I was startled when she pulled away and opened her door.

"Come on, Butch, join me in the backseat. I wanna see what you're made of."

I've never felt that same electric shock of anticipation and pure terror in any encounter I've had since that moment. I'd been with other girls before, but always ones about as experienced as I was, which is to say, not very. I knew the basics of having sex with a girl, but she was nothing like any of them, except in the strictest biological sense. Her experience and confidence intimidated the hell out of me. I was terrified I'd do something wrong, and at the same time beside myself with excitement over having a chance with her.

I nearly fell out of the car in my haste. She laughed and pulled me into the back so fast I landed across her in an ungainly heap. So far I wasn't very impressed with myself and I was sure she'd change her mind at any moment, realizing the foolhardiness of her impulsive choice. Lucky for me, she didn't seem turned off by my clumsiness.

She wrapped one arm around my shoulder and brought my face close to hers. I almost lost my limited cool right there, looking into her eyes, her lips open and moist. Fortunately, even in a situation of extreme nervousness with a gorgeous woman, I can manage a kiss. And damn, damn, damn...I'll never forget her lips, full and firm but giving in at just the right moments. Her tongue teasing and tormenting mine until it followed hers.

I have no idea how much time we spent just making out, but it was glorious and I was in no hurry to get to the next base.

She was a bit more motivated, judging by the way she broke our lip-lock, pressed me back against the seat and straddled my lap. We were still fully clothed but I could feel the heat of her mound as it pressed against mine. I reached around, grabbing her ass, pulling her more firmly against me. She sucked on my neck and ears as we rocked against each other, occasionally visiting my mouth for deep, searing kisses. When she wasn't pressing her lips against mine, or moaning, there was a steady stream of dirty words coming out of her mouth that both impressed and encouraged me. I lifted my pelvis a little more, grabbed her ass and held her tightly against me. She gasped, rubbing even faster, pressing against my clit and bringing me to the brink of orgasm in seconds. I groaned from deep in my belly, a counterpoint to her higher cry of pleasure.

She slid over into the seat next to me and we both took a moment to catch our breath. "Mmmm, that was a good ride, Butch. I sure hope you've got more in the tank, 'cause I'm not through with you." She reached between my legs and gave me a squeeze. "You're not done, are you?"

I smiled. If there's one thing I'd learned in the few sexual relationships I'd had, it was that "done" wasn't in my body's vocabulary. I reached over to stroke her through the thin fabric of her chinos, wet with the telltale results of her climax.

"I don't know this word *done*." I was feeling confident and high. "Can you show me what you mean?"

She laughed, delighted by my response and, possibly, my cockiness. What followed were several rounds of us showing off our best moves and a few others we improvised on the spot. If you've ever had sex in the backseat of a compact car, you'll remember how inconveniently placed the door handles are, and the way seat belt buckles can impale your backside, and the way you can't straighten your legs or figure out where your feet are supposed to go. In the moment, though, the only parts of my body I was aware of were the ones she was touching.

At one point, despite the impossibly cramped space, she went down on me. I do not, to this day, know where she put the rest of her body, but when her tongue lapped my clit, I ceased worrying about it. It felt like someone had connected a live electrical wire directly to my veins. I practically levitated off the car seat. And though I wasn't necessarily done, I needed a moment afterward to pause and take it all in. She looked up at me with a big, proud grin.

"You liked that a lot, didn't ya, Butch?"

"Oh my god, oh my god, what...how...?"

Laughing, she pulled herself up to my face and kissed me. "So you want to know what I did?"

"Yes, please."

"Stick out your tongue."

"Uh, what?"

"Stick out your tongue and I'll show you what I was doing."

I did as I was told. She flicked the tip of her tongue upward against mine, like plucking a guitar string, and continued, flicking rapidly, then slowing down and circling the tip. My clit throbbed with the memory of it. She began to stroke my tongue with hers, and then swept around the circle of my lips. I groaned, pressing my hips against her where she was perched on my lap. She gave me a full kiss, her tongue wrapping itself around mine, teasing it back out of my mouth. She pressed her lips around the tip of my tongue and sucked on it, occasionally flicking the underside. I groaned and grabbed her hips, thrusting hard against her. She responded by taking more of my tongue into her mouth and grinding herself against me. I came hard and loud, banging my fist against the back of the passenger seat, my voice partially muffled against her mouth.

We were out until the first rosy blush of dawn began to show against the horizon. When I finally dropped myself into bed, I was simultaneously exhilarated and exhausted to my very bones. I skipped my morning classes, sleeping until my roommate woke me up by playing her crappy music too loud, somewhere in the vicinity of noon. I was still groggy, eyes full of sand and brain feeling like mush, when I remembered the night before and, with a jolt, remembered she and I would be working together again that night. Adrenaline straightened me up better than coffee and I went through the rest of my day in a horny daze.

The weeks and months that followed are mostly a blur in my memory. I didn't sleep much and there were a lot of late nights. I looked for any opportunity to work the closing shift with her, trading with others and taking doubles if someone called in sick. She continued to tutor me in the fine art of pleasuring a woman as we toured the county, finding interesting and out-of-the-way places to have sex in her car.

As amazingly skilled as she was with her tongue, she was even better with her fingers. On one occasion, after she'd reduced me to a spent husk struggling to regain my breath, I asked her, "What was that? How did you do that?"

"Uh-huh, you liked that, I could tell. You nearly broke my hand when you came." She moved up my body to rest her head on my shoulder, and held her hand out as if she were going to do a shadow puppet show. "I had my thumb in your ass, like this." She wiggled her thumb and my ass clenched in response. "And I had two fingers in your cunt, like this." She made a running in place motion with her first and second fingers and I clenched even harder. "But before that, I had my thumb circling your clit, like this." She switched her hand position and her thumb circled a spot in the air. My clit throbbed and I moaned. "And my fingers were stroking your G-spot, like this." More running

in place motions and I lifted my hips and pulled her thigh down
between my legs and rutted until I'd come again.

As I collapsed a second time, she laughed, kissing my chest.
"Oh my god, Butch, you are so easy. You're so much fun to play
with."

At work, she was still shamelessly flirting with everyone,
coworkers and customers alike. And when we were alone, she'd
pull me into the back, out of sight. She'd push me up against a
wall or the dishwasher and grind against my thigh, then slide
her fingers between us and press them against the seam of my
pants. We became experts in coming quickly and quietly. We
almost got caught once, when a regular customer came in a
little later than usual and poked his head around the corner,
calling out to see if anyone was around. At the sound of his
voice, I turned away quickly and reached up as if to get a can of
olives and she hustled out to make his sandwich.

She only invited me to her apartment a few times, when her
roommate was away. My dorm room was cramped and I shared
it with a loud, obnoxious roommate, so I didn't criticize the
arrangement. Her car became our refuge, a comfortable cocoon,
shielding us from prying eyes and the cold night air.

After months of being pulled into dark corners and kissed
until I was breathless, I finally got the nerve to return the favor.
She was getting stock in the back room when I came up from
behind, wrapping my arms around her and pulling her tightly
against me. My voice was suave and confident in her ear. "Hey,
hot stuff, let's close early and go see what I'm made of." It was
my attempt at being sexy and hot and everything she had been
for me. She turned, looked me up and down in an appraising
way, noting my cocky smile and the confidence in my eyes.

"Okay, stud, let's get out of here."

It was a roll in the backseat like the ones before, but something had definitely changed between us. I wasn't waiting for her

to make the first move. I came on strong and gave her a tour of all the skills I'd learned from her. At the end of it, she sat on my lap, both of us wrapped in a blanket, the car's fogged windows a second comforting layer, the night deep and still around us. She looked up at me, face very serious and almost sad. She stroked my cheek and gave me a tender, loving kiss. We'd been making out for months, but she'd never kissed me like that before. It was much more intimate than fucking. There was an openness and vulnerability in her that I hadn't felt before. We'd always been strictly casual, never getting serious about what we were doing, never talking about the future or our feelings for each other. I was flush with emotion and high on sex, and with that kiss fresh on my lips, I came close to telling her how I really felt. I got as far as "I luh..." before she stopped me, putting her hand lightly across my mouth.

"Come on now, Butch, let's not get all serious and ruin our fun." Her words were light, but there was a warning in her eyes.

"Oh, well, I was only gonna say, 'I luh...like you, a lot.'" I attempted a light and dismissive laugh. I was trying to play it cool, but I could feel embarrassment on my cheeks and a nauseous feeling in my stomach. It was way more than "like" and in that moment, I knew I'd fallen for her far more than she had for me. I guess I should have known better; she was very clear about not wanting commitment. Looking back now, I can see I was in massive denial. I thought I could be the one, the one who could change her mind, the one she'd finally settle down with.

After that night things were the same, but different. We still fooled around in the back room, with me initiating more and more. We still had incredible amounts of sex and I was still discovering parts of the county I never knew existed. She kissed me just as hard and we still fucked just as thoroughly. But even though she started opening up more to me, sharing more about her life, there was a tension between us that hadn't been there before. The lighthearted playfulness that had always been so easy was harder to find. Even though I hadn't uttered the L-word, it was always there, hanging between us. I'd fallen in love with her. Things had gotten more serious between us, as much as we both tried to deny it.

We didn't break up as much as we drifted apart. I had to start paying more attention to my college courses and she found other things to do while I was busy studying. I began to admit to myself that it was easier to be away from her than to be with her and know she didn't love me the way I loved her. I won't pretend it didn't hurt like hell the first time I saw her with someone else, but by then there was a girl in my program who'd gotten my attention and I was trying to figure out how to get hers.

I took a deep breath and returned to the present. My friend, who'd been listening intently, reached out to take one of my hands between hers.

"That's such a sad ending. I'm really sorry."

I welcomed the gesture, not the least because I'd been hoping to get to know her better. Her hands were warm and a promising frisson of energy passed between us when we touched. She shared some traits with the girl in the story. She was gorgeous, very direct about what she wanted and had a way of smiling at me that made my insides come undone. Unlike my sandwich-shop girl, this woman was warm and generous and seemed open to the possibility of a deeper relationship.

"Well, it wasn't all bad. We had a lot of good times, and great sex. I certainly learned a lot from her." I raised my eyebrows suggestively.

My friend smiled a little wickedly and looked at me from under her lashes. "Mmm...she taught you a lot of tricks, did she? Anything you'd care to pass on to a...friend?"

I returned her smile. "Seems the least I could do, as a friend."

I moved closer to her on the couch, resting my hand on her thigh. She reached over to stroke the short hairs on the back of my neck.

Again, that wicked smile. "So, stud, you gonna show me what you're made of?"

WELDER BOI

Axa Lee

Why be a boi on a farm?" I asked her once. "Wouldn't it be easier to just be a lesbian?"

She snorted. "Have you ever tried being a woman on a farm?" She slammed the drawer of the big toolbox shut, making me jump.

"I'm not asking them to think of me as another gender, just as something other than 'Harold Milford's daughter.' It shouldn't matter if I have a cock or not, just as long as I do good work."

Gender is the only thing fluid about her. In the rest, she is metal and flame.

"But you didn't want to be butch?"

She rolled her eyes at me. "Why do you have to label everything?"

We got back to this often, and she already knew the answer. Gays label everything, in my opinion, all the while insisting on the limitations of labels. Bitches be cray, I tell her, and that's why we love them.

With a sharp nod of her head, she tipped the welding helmet over her eyes and sparked her rod.

I love watching her weld. She ties that bandana around her cropped blonde hair, tips that helmet down with a sharp motion of her chin, her spark ignites, and she's nothing but liquid flame. She's an artist, a true creative. Though she laughs when I tell her this and says she's only welding fence posts.

Sweat drips down her back beneath the leather protective gear, her arms are veined and strong beneath those heavy gloves, her leather boots with the steel toes peeking through… there's just nothing that isn't sexy.

She comes to me later, stripped down to her white wife-beater and favorite battered jeans that ride low-slung across her narrow hips, so worn they're as soft as a T-shirt, her muscular chest almost as flat as a boy's, a real boy's. She's not one for labels and laughed when I told her what hers was, then pulled me across her lap and kissed me, the scent of steel and fire wafting between us.

There's always a tang of fire in her hair, a breath of metal about her, as if she took the elements of her craft into herself and continued to exude them. Or was made of them all along.

She doesn't believe in feng shui or astrology, so when I talk to her of elements, of water signs and fire signs, of dragons, wood or Taurus, she rolls her eyes and lets her beer bottle dangle between her fingertips.

"Dialing psychic hotline, Crazy speaking." She holds her fingers like a phone, thumb to ear and pinkie to mouth.

I read her palm once, traced the heart line, the lifeline, and explained that the squared tips of her fingers and close nails meant she was a very practical person.

"You've met me, right?" she said. "Is there any way to describe me other than practical?" She laughed and cupped the back of my head, bending me in for a kiss.

"Just let it be, Jess," she said.

But, as she said, she's met me. I can't let it be.

I'm tending my herbs in the south room, shifting them from window to window in the makeshift sunroom until next fall when we renovate and can add bigger windows for more light. I'm so absorbed in pruning my ailing aloe plant that I don't hear her come in. Her voice startles me out of the plant haze I've lost myself in.

"What does this card mean?" she asks.

I jerk and my eyes fall to the tarot spread I've left on the only clean space available on my worktable. I repot all my plants there, but this morning, while sipping my coffee, I did a spread. The cup still sat beside the cards that lay faceup in a classic Celtic cross pattern.

"The page of cups," I say. "For you."

She doesn't look up at me, merely studies the spread. "And this one?"

She points to the card crossing her significator, the one that indicates present circumstances.

"The hanged man," I tell her, "for attaining wisdom."

She nods. "And this one?" She points to the tower card, four cards away from the next one in the reading.

I shake my head. "This one," I correct her, and point to the next card in the reading, the one that strengthens or weakens the first card. "The queen of cups. For happiness and"—I grin at her—"wise choices in relationships."

She rolls her eyes. I ignore her and point to the next card. "Your goals, the nine of cups, a very good card. All you want will come to pass." I'm warming up now, liking how she's listening to me, nodding, intent on the reading, as though if she squints at the cards hard enough she'll be able to divine them for herself. "The world, meaning you understand the world around you, and how you came to be here. The tower, something disrupted your life for a while…"

"Gee, big surprise there," she muttered. We'd talked a lot about what coming out as not just a lesbian but as a boi, a term virtually no one knew about, meant in a closed, northern farm community like the one she lived in.

"…But didn't mean the end. This next card, it tells you what to expect, what you can look forward to—"

But she doesn't let me finish. She lays her hand over mine and suddenly we're close. I feel her entire body along the backside of mine. I don't remember how this happened. One moment we were across the room from each other, now we're nearly touching. I can't control how my body reacts to her as she speaks this last, her breath trailing down the column of my neck, her words moving within me as if she stroked me with her voice. I close my eyes against the force of the immediate and violently visceral physical reaction. My pulse races, I'm suddenly wet, as the smell of her, the tang of metal, the sharp puff of flame, like a burnt-out candle, burns through me with the jolt of immediacy akin to being shocked by an electric fence.

"You," she says. Her voice is husky; it sounds like it does after she's been welding all day, breathing smoke and fire, like a confused dragon, breathing it in instead of out. "I can look forward to you."

"It's…it's…" But I can't answer. And I can't let it be. I can't do anything as she caresses the side my neck with her fingers first, followed by her mouth, lingering in the way she knows I like, drawing out the sensations so that when I finally open my eyes after she pulls away I know it will take several seconds for my eyes to refocus.

In almost one motion, she jerks down my cutoffs and panties. It's too hot for niceties, too hot for making love; this is sex, raw lust. We need each other, badly, that connection of spirit through flesh. And we'll both take what we need, giving back that much and more.

She grabs my hips and sets me up on the worktable. The cards scatter. She's deceptively strong, wiry, all lean muscle from long hours in the forge.

She spreads my legs before her on the counter, hands resting on my knees to keep them apart. And without preamble, she bends her head and uses the thickest part of her tongue to lick me, from the bottom of my slit to my clit. I arch my back and shake, gripping her shoulders for an anchor, before I'm lost to the bliss of her mouth on my cunt.

I'm not feeling the hard tabletop beneath my ass anymore or thinking about how anyone driving up the driveway can see me, legs spread wide, fingers tangled in her sweat-spiked blonde hair as she pleasures me with mouth, lips and fingers. The smell of crushed lemon balm and basil is in my nose, and I can't catch my breath.

She rims my slit with her tongue, stabbing into me with enough suddenness to make my head fall back in ecstasy. My pussy is so wet and swollen—every time I think she has me as wet as she ever has, she ups the ante.

I love the strong length of her back. It's displayed as she bends beneath me, the play of muscles beneath pale skin, and the point where farmer's tan meets the natural alabaster of her own skin. For me, she embodies strength, the juncture where masculine and feminine merge, making me feel both protected and nurtured, spinning in my head until it all jumbles and all I feel is her.

She's not soft. She's the very opposite of soft. Not to say that she's unyielding; she's simply everything that is not soft. She's strong. She's firm. She's all hard angles and tough resolve. No, there is nothing soft about my boi.

I worry about being the kind of girl who's soft. I often think she'll someday want someone as solid as she is. I worry that she'll stop valuing my creativity and zest for life and want someone more grounded. I worry the contradiction of our own natures will be the rock our love breaks itself against. The psychology grad student in me wants to unravel her, to untangle all her motivations and dichotomies, while the lover in me only wants to hold her close.

She strokes my nether lips with her tongue, sending a shock straight through me. It doesn't matter how many times we do this, I react to her instantaneously, as I never have with anyone else. She plays it cool and controlled, but I know that beneath that cool exterior, she's just as affected as I am.

I rake my nails over the upper part of her back and drag her white wife-beater up and off over her head. Where city bois might opt for breast binding at the least, double mastectomy at the most extreme, where my breasts would spring free, Natalie's remain tightly pulled up to her chest, the nipples rigid twists of flesh against an almost board-flat chest. Her nipples are pink and tiny, nubs of tightly puckered flesh that I love to flick my tongue against. Those same city bois would spike their hair with gel, trying to look sophisticated, or soph, whereas at the end of the day her hair is spiked by dried sweat and soot.

They're different animals, those bois and mine. Or maybe this is just the image of a country boi.

As I said, dykes like me love labels.

But there's so much fluidity to a label.

I flick my tongue over the intensely sensitive nub of her nipple until she shivers. I bite a little then, nipping her with my teeth. She likes pain more than I do. It gets her off faster than anything. Dripping wax on her bare skin gets her hotter than I can explain.

She groans, pressing into me for a moment, almost yielding to my teeth, before thrusting me so that I lie back on the table.

She slides her hands beneath my ass and my legs go over her shoulders and her mouth is on me again and I can't contain the cry that escapes me. Our fucking is raw and real and the closest thing to a religious experience I ever hope to encounter.

I feel the pressure building, that deep weight in my pelvis, those tingling jolts shooting outward from deep in my belly. But I'm not ready yet.

And suddenly, with the scent of crushed peppermint and lavender in my nose, I realize, with the greatest clarity, that there's nothing to unravel here—boi, grrl, dyke, butch—there're only two people, in love with each other.

I shove against her, sit up and drag her to the floor with me. I need her mouth on mine, I need to look into her eyes, I need to hold her as I come.

We roll and writhe against each other on the floor, amidst the spilled potting soil and dried, dead leaves. Her hand is on my pussy, her fingers taking the place of her mouth. Our tongues mesh against each other, warring for space, teeth striking and parting, as her fingers alternately tease my clit and thrust inside, stroking my G-spot. She has me on the edge again, rolling and spinning in pleasure, writhing and grunting, barely feeling human anymore, nothing but sensation, throbbing with lust.

As she brings me closer, those jolts suddenly exploding within me, like warm whiskey glaze made electric, I cling to her, babbling nonsense. She holds me, clutches me, presses her face into my neck and hair, letting me know that she will never let me go. And as I come, I look up at her, meeting her eyes. And I notice her eyes.

They're soft.

For me.

I'm shaking. I can't seem to stop. She slides up my body and suspends herself above me, our foreheads the only thing touching above the tangle of our legs.

"I fucking love you," she says. "You know that right?"

"I know, baby," I murmur. "I love you too."

She crushes me to her, pelvis to pelvis, breast to breast, rolls us onto our sides and hugs me like she'll never let me go. I hope she never does.

TEAMWORK

Dena Hankins

Sun baked the concrete pier and heat seeped into the boat shed, abandoned and echoing on Labor Day. Tilly shifted the wide straps of her sports bra. They cut into the muscle she'd put on for the racing season.

"Come on, Tilly, don't just stand there." Spin stood next to her, legs spread.

"Yeah, yeah. Hold your horses. We're supposed to stretch between sets."

"You weren't stretching. You were playing with your bra." Spin nudged Tilly with a sweaty elbow.

Tilly rolled her eyes and set up for the two-person rope pull. She leaned back against Spin's pull, letting the rope out slowly, and watched Spin's triceps flex at each push backward. She increased the resistance to make Spin work harder and sighed at the shifting muscles in Spin's arms. Envy and desire, and nothing to do about either one.

When Tilly reached the end of the rope, they switched jobs. Tilly pulled against Spin's resistance and her upper lip rose in a sneer of effort. The forward arm had the easy job. It was the push backward that fucked her up every time. Sweat ran down her temples and her shirt clung to her back. Her stroke shortened and Spin barked, "All the way back." Tilly pushed harder and her sneer turned into grunts of effort. After ten sets each, with a different arm forward each time, Spin pulled the rope free with a flourish. She walked to the ceiling beam with as much swagger as ever, but Tilly was gratified to see that her shirt was soaked in sweat too.

Tilly hooked her fingers on the pillar and stretched out her chest, watching Spin toss the line over the ceiling beam and pull into her own stretch. Arms flung wide and eyes closed, Spin leaned forward, pulling both arms back. Tilly's mouth went dry at the sight of her bunched shoulders, lean arms and the slight curve under the front of her shirt. When Spin twisted her hips to stretch her back and sides and belly, Tilly's mouth was the only dry part of her body.

Sweating even harder than a moment ago and wondering if she was wet enough to soak through her tight running shorts, Tilly turned around and hooked the pillar with the fingers of her other hand. She twisted away from the post, feeling the warmth and ache in her bicep and pecs. She enjoyed stretching more than working out.

A hot hand grabbed her wrist and Tilly jerked. Spin's arm came around her waist and drew her a tiny bit farther from the pillar. Breath arrested, Tilly stiffened.

Before she could sort through her confusion enough to respond, before she had a clue how she wanted to respond, Spin released her. "Just touch with the ends of your fingers and turn farther away. That way you stretch your hand and your forearm along with the rest."

Cold disappointment turned into embarrassment and rage. Spin's touch had torched Tilly's body like a cigarette thrown from a car during a drought and she had to have felt the quiver.

Running a racing sailboat required a cool head, but that cool was nowhere to be found now. Fair or not, Tilly ached to fist her hands and lay into Spin for teasing her. She vibrated with the urge to grab Spin and jerk her close. Tilly whirled around, snarling. She didn't know what was going to happen when she looked Spin in the face.

Spin was walking away, already several steps from Tilly.

She swallowed her anger. For the best, anyway. She prized the work they did together and the way they excelled as a team. On the boat, Tilly called the shots and Spin scrambled. Off the boat, Spin ran team training, her wiry build and sheer energy giving her an edge on strength. Their nicknames—Tilly for the tiller she never released and Spin for the big spinnaker sail she handled so deftly—were so natural that even their families back home had adopted them.

As she'd done so often before, Tilly shoved her attraction aside. She finished her exercises, stretched her way back to serenity, then sat up tall on a mat and pulled her feet together in front of her, sole to sole. She felt grounded, much better. A couple of feet away, Spin finished her own stretches and leaned back on her hands.

"Why did you freeze up when I touched you?"

Tilly closed her eyes and sighed. The pleasant hum of her hard-worked body continued in the background, but the vast and hard-won emptiness in her mind began to teem with questions and emotions. "I don't know what you're talking about."

"Yes, you do. We've crewed together for three years and I've never made a move on you. Do you think I would fuck with our partnership by trying to push you into anything?"

Tilly opened her eyes. Spin sounded calm, but tension pulled her mouth flat. "You're really upset about this?" Her voice expressed mild curiosity. Tilly decided she was proud of herself for holding it together in the face of the topic she'd hoped to avoid forever.

"Damn right I'm upset. Don't sit there like you are above it all. I felt your body tighten. Your belly turned hard as rock. And that's saying something."

Tilly narrowed her eyes at Spin. "Are you seriously making a crack about my weight?"

"Shut up." Spin sighed. "You know that's not what I was saying."

"What are you saying?"

"I'm saying…" Spin struggled for words. Tilly had never seen Spin struggle for anything that wasn't physical. She softened at Spin's discomfort.

"Don't worry about it. Nothing happened."

"No!" Spin sat forward. Tilly was surprised by the vehemence of the denial. "I'm tired of tiptoeing around the subject with you, Tilly. We're going to have it out, once and for all."

"Have what out?" Tilly was bewildered. In the nightmares where she made a move on Spin and got brushed off, it never went like this. "What are you talking about?"

"I won't lie and say I'm not attracted to you, Tilly. I've always wished we could give it a try, but you mean too much to me for a fling. Sometimes you seem to respond to me, but it never lasts. You always pull away. This season has been worse than ever. It feels like you don't want me anywhere near you! It's a small boat, Tilly. I can accept if you don't want me, but you have to know you're safe with me."

Tilly sat blinking, still holding her ankles in front of her on the mat. Spin's words didn't fit. Where was this coming from? They'd ended up at some of the same college parties and usually stuck together on out-of-town trips, but their closeness evaporated away from the docks. With all the countless hours they'd spent together, they'd never once sat around and shot the shit with a drink in hand, let alone hinted at more.

Spin kept her eyes trained steadily on Tilly's face until Tilly spoke. "I know I'm safe with you."

Spin tightened her lips and looked away. "I guess that's good enough, then." She brushed her hands against each other and rocked as though to stand up.

"Wait!" Tilly felt the moment slipping away and realized that she had to know what Spin meant by her words. "You're talking nonsense, Spin. You've never been attracted to me. You like high femmes. Fingernails and makeup." Tilly heard her own words and knew them to be false. Or, if not false, at least only partly true. Spin had dated most of the lesbians at school and an eyebrow-raising number of straight girls. Some decided they were bi and others went back to guys afterward, but none of them ever talked bad about Spin when it was over.

Waving her hands in front of her, Tilly wordlessly asked for a moment of silence.

Spin acquiesced, but a quirk at the corner of her mouth suggested that she was taking stock, just as Tilly was. When Tilly finally spoke again, she said, "I'm confused, Spin. I thought you were completely uninterested in me. You never invited me to parties or asked me out. And don't say that goes both ways. You and I both know your style. You've never been slow to ask out any girl who interested you."

"Any girl but you." Spin's quiet response liquefied Tilly's belly in some strange way. "I wasn't even sure you were queer at first. Maybe just a tomboy? And then you started dating Mag…"

"Unbelievable." Tilly rose to her knees and crawled closer to Spin. "If you're saying what I think you're saying…I don't want to feel safe from you. I want more than that."

Tilly grabbed the back of Spin's head and held it while she touched their lips together, then pressed. She felt the tip of Spin's tongue and opened her mouth to touch it with her own. The sensation of slick and rough combined pulled her deeper into the kiss. When Spin gripped Tilly's ribs, Tilly swung a leg over and sat astride her lap. In a fever, they kissed deeply, endlessly, inhaling the sweat and salt that covered their faces, licking at each other's teeth and lips and tongues.

When Tilly was able to process a thought again, it was that Spin had to be uncomfortable. She raised her head to speak, but Spin stole her breath by pressing her face to the tightly bound cleavage under Tilly's team shirt. She ran her hands down Tilly's sides and around her ass. Tilly had a fraction of a second to anticipate before the reality of Spin's hands, gripping the tender curve firmly, overwhelmed imagination. Spin pulled Tilly closer, hard against her flexed belly, and breathed deeply.

Spin raised her head. "I don't know where this will go, but I want to fuck you so bad right now."

Tilly melted and her cunt flexed. "There's no one around."

Spin rocked back slowly, strong abs controlling their fall, eyes fixed on Tilly's. Tilly gave in to the pull of her arms and followed her down. She drew up tight when Spin groaned at the press of Tilly's breasts against hers. Tilly held part of her weight on her forearms and rocked her hips against the narrower span of Spin's.

Spin planted a foot and twisted, taking Tilly down onto her back. Looming over her from the side, Spin groaned. "You are so fucking sexy."

"I smell like a locker room," Tilly complained.

"You smell great." Spin ran her hand down Tilly's belly to her hip and pulled. Their bellies met, side to side, and they kissed, hard-handed on each other's hips. It wasn't nearly enough and Tilly pushed upright. Spin rose to her knees, looming, and pulled Tilly's shirt up and off. Tilly pushed Spin's shirt up and dove in to lick the skin between her small breasts while Spin dispensed with the garment, scraping the sports bra off over her head in one quick motion.

Tilly pressed Spin's shoulders back and got a first good look at her, topless. Her muscled arms and shoulders softened at her high breasts, with their shallow curve off her ribs. Her waist dipped in from her narrow ribs and Tilly could see her hip bones pressing outward just over the waistband of her low exercise pants. Spin never dressed to hide her shape, but it was different, seeing her without wrapping. She looked touchable, pleasurable, where before, Tilly hadn't been able to imagine what Spin would want from a lover. Looking at her bullet-hard nipples, Tilly thought it was a good bet that Spin would respond violently to having them stimulated.

"Come on," Spin begged. "Take off your bra." She knelt back on her heels, watching with rapt attention as Tilly performed the acrobatic maneuver of removing a damp, too-small sports bra from a large-breasted frame. Not a process she ordinarily thought of as sexy, but Spin's expression let Tilly know that it turned her on. She stretched the reinforced bottom hem up and over her breasts, inching the band up all the way around. When she crossed her arms and pulled upward on the bunched-up bra, Spin's face went slack and her hands twitched. It barely cleared Tilly's head before Spin attacked.

Strong, rough hands closed over Tilly's heavy breasts. They hung down somewhat and then curved outward in a swoop that ended at her small, crinkled nipples. Tilly sighed at the relief of pressure and the ache of her nipples' release from their cage.

"I can't believe you keep these things packed away." Spin massaged the deep, vivid lines left by the sports bra and kissed the indentation on Tilly's shoulder. "I'll never tease you about playing with your bra again."

Tilly laughed. "Ah, but it feels so good when I set them free."

"Breast bondage?" Spin's caresses moved from therapeutic to arousing.

"No, not really. It just takes a lot of pressure to hold them in place. Oh, that's nice."

Spin smiled and pulled Tilly up so that they knelt with thighs and breasts pressed hard against one another. Tilly grabbed Spin's shoulders, strong muscle over delicate bone, and pulled her closer. She licked the small collarbone and shoved Spin hard, wanting to get her on her back where she could put her hands all over her. Spin shoved back, taking Tilly by surprise. She arched over Tilly, bowing her back and lifting a tight nipple to her mouth. The gnawing, pulling feeling made Tilly's hands spasm on Spin's shoulders, less to keep from tipping over backward and more to make sure the other couldn't move away.

Spin raised one knee, planting her foot beside Tilly's hip and effectively imprisoning her within the cage of her arms and knee. Suddenly overwhelmed, Tilly pushed upward, shoving her chest into Spin's. Their workout shorts slid against each other when Tilly got one foot under her.

Spin growled. "Give it to me."

Tilly laughed shortly and tossed back with bravado, "Take it, if you can."

Spin pushed forward and Tilly matched her pressure. Burning muscles protested the contest, but Tilly refused to give Spin the right to run the fuck. At least, not without a fight. Swaying back and forth with the intensity of their press together, Tilly reached around and grabbed Spin's tight ass, then slapped her asscheeks. The moment of surprise froze Spin, and Tilly heaved against her.

Spin counterattacked with a shove upward that brought them both to their feet, scrabbling for footing. She wrapped one arm around Tilly's waist, the slide of rough skin on soft wrenching a moan from them both. The other hand went to Tilly's nape and Tilly threw herself into the kiss. They kissed deeply, mouths open, panting. Tilly's hands roamed Spin's back, gripping, scratching. She wanted inside, all the way in.

Overworked muscles burned with fierce pleasure. Swaying into each other, pushing and pulling hard, every wrestling grip was massage and caress. Tilly searched Spin's firm ass, trying to get closer, then plunged her hands inside, down the back of her pants. The sweaty, sticky skin triggered madness in her and Tilly lifted Spin and threw her onto the mat with a strength that took them both by surprise. She followed her down and stripped Spin's pants and underwear to her knees. Tilly fastened her mouth to Spin's nipple and plunged her free hand into her pubic hair.

Spin made a noise that Tilly had never heard before. It was the hoarse plea of a woman catapulted past thought into pure physicality, a scream and a groan, all at once. And when Tilly drew hard on the nipple in her mouth, Spin made the noise again and again. Cupping the bone and soft flesh of Spin's cunt, Tilly reveled in her control. This was Spin in her mouth, her strong scent filling her nose.

Tilly's fingers turned slippery before she even nudged apart Spin's labia, so wet that Tilly's fingers sank into the gap without hesitation. She lapped at her nipple, tugged and sucked on it, and switched to the other when Spin writhed. A single finger made the rounds, finding the entry to her cunt, the irregular and thin inner lips, and, right where they met, a firm and protuberant clit. The smile that came broke the suction of mouth on nipple and Tilly nipped at the under-curve of Spin's breast while she began to stroke.

Spin panted, grabbing at Tilly's shoulder and gripping her arm. Tilly leaned up to kiss Spin again and they shared breath, open mouths together but not engaged. Looking into her eyes, Tilly asked Spin, "Where do you want my mouth?"

Spin moaned at the relentless stroking of Tilly's fingers and answered, "On my tits."

With an understanding smile, Tilly gave up the hope of going down on her this time. She put her mouth back to work, sucking and biting and pulling Spin's nipples. Tilly found an angle from which she could get her fingers inside Spin's cunt to the first couple of knuckles without leaving her clit alone. Tilly groaned against Spin's breast at the give in her soft tissues, the stretch and softness and streaming wetness.

Pulling hard on one nipple made Spin's cunt flex and circling over her clit at the same time made it clench. Tilly rose on one knee over Spin. Her second hand freed, she created a rhythm between her hands and mouth that echoed the rocking of Spin's hips and the arching of her back. Spin panted and groaned, increasing the speed of her movements, taut muscles working in her belly. Tilly followed her lead, fucking her faster and harder until Spin was tearing at her shoulders with her frantic grip. Tilly's overworked biceps protested at the demand, but the pain disappeared when Spin froze.

A slight pulsing of Spin's belly and hands warned Tilly not to stop. Spin would come if she kept going. The pause felt like the moment at the top of a roller coaster and Tilly wanted to push harder, fuck Spin over the edge. She felt Spin's clit draw up and then she exploded in convulsive trembling that rolled from deep in her cunt to her limbs and out her fingers and toes. Tilly lightened her touch but kept the pace and milked every last shudder from Spin's dynamic body.

Resting her forehead on Spin's belly, Tilly smoothed the swollen flesh she'd rubbed so hard. Breathing deeply, she controlled the urge to roll on top of Spin and rub herself to orgasm. It wouldn't take long, for damn sure. Her nerves were honed, making her aware of the mat under her, the dusty smell of the boat shed, but mostly of the heat radiating from Spin.

Spin's body tightened under Tilly and launched over her in a quick flip. Tilly reveled in being under Spin and arched into her body.

Looking up at Spin's slumberous eyes, Tilly gave a cat's-cream smile. "Oh, now you can pin me."

Spin matched the smile and kissed Tilly lightly on the lips, then her cheek, then her chin. She licked Tilly's salty neck and raised her cunt-slick hand to lick that too. Spin draped Tilly's arms on the mat over her head and stroked her sides.

"So you think you won?"

Tilly stretched under the long, slow sweep of Spin's hand. "Mmm-hmm." Her eyes drifted closed.

Spin's hands went back to Tilly's upraised arms, grasping her firmly at the wrist. "Next time, there won't be any mercy."

Tilly opened her eyes. "Tell yourself whatever makes you feel better, honey."

She could feel Spin's mouth move in a smile. "Don't move," Spin instructed. She breathed deep between Tilly's upthrust breasts and stroked the curve of them with her nose, then nuzzled around the bottom and breathed deep in Tilly's armpit. When Tilly flinched, Spin repeated her command. "Don't move." She released Tilly's wrists to run a hand along the tender underside of her arm and down her side, then inhaled again. "You smell like work. You smell like woman." Nibbling up her breast, she said, "I love your smell. It's always turned me on when we work out together."

Tilly squirmed, half-ticklish and half-disbelieving. She left her arms up, though, and Spin rewarded her with a question. Speaking with her chin on Tilly's breastbone, Spin asked, "Where would you like my mouth?"

Tilly's belly quivered and Spin smiled. After a false start, Tilly managed to answer, "On my pussy."

Spin pressed Tilly's breasts together and kissed each nipple before releasing them and moving down. Tilly spread her legs at Spin's touch and her fingers scrabbled for a hold on the slick mat.

She planted her heels and arched into Spin, who didn't tease her. One hand slid under her ass to keep her hips up and the other spread her pussy lips. Tilly quaked at the feeling of hot tongue directly on her clit and spread her arms to either side as though that might stabilize her. Spin licked and sucked at Tilly's clit. It felt huge, and Tilly pumped her hips, imagining it thrusting deep into Spin's mouth. Spin settled into a pursed-lipped suction, letting Tilly pump her clit against Spin's tongue.

She didn't try to control her hunger or her body's reaction. Her hips started making crazy circles and Spin worked one and then two fingers into Tilly's pussy. It felt like a lot when she clenched, but she opened up for each finger that Spin presented. Pressing forward until Tilly could feel her second knuckles at the opening of her pussy, Spin curved her fingers forward to the spot that made Tilly cry out loud, and held her fingers there. Tilly bounced and circled her hips, sobbing wildly at the double tap of clit and G-spot. Spin kept her tongue soft and her lips tight, her fingers poised, and every move Tilly made battered her against the wall of Spin's inescapable stimulation. Tilly wound tighter and tighter until Spin's fingers were squeezed so hard they ground against one another. Blood pounded in Tilly's head as she saw a flash of white and felt the universe take one large step sideways. The rhythmic clench and release of her cunt was echoed throughout her body and softened along with the rest of her sore, heavy muscles when she sighed and let go.

Spin pressed her lips to Tilly's pubic bone before sliding up and lying full length on her. Tilly tasted herself on Spin's wet mouth, her body throbbing, spent with the combined exertions of working out and fucking.

Tilly's only coherent thought came slow and lazy. They'd both wanted this, all along. It came as no surprise that sex between them was off the charts.

Sailing isn't the only thing that's all about teamwork.

DANCING BOI

Kathleen Tudor

When Tara invited me to her bachelorette party, I simply sighed and chalked it up as yet another stupid event I had to show up for in the name of office harmony. I expected to be bored. I expected to have to fake interest in a barely concealed cock or two. I did not expect the curveball she threw me.

"Blake and I have decided not to tempt ourselves, but that doesn't mean we can't still have fun," she said.

"But…"

"Think of it as an adventure! It's going to be great. We'll pretend we're that kind of wild girl for one night. Be brave!"

"I don't think—"

"Please? Come on, it'll be fun! I'm going to bring a whole bunch of ones and dare everybody to give them to the strippers." She made puppy eyes at me, and I clenched my jaw. In the name of not trusting each other, apparently, she and her husband-to-be had agreed: strippers were okay, but only if they were same-sex strippers. The guys got Chippendales or nothing, and we girls… well, we were hitting a nice, traditional strip joint. Problem was, none of the girls from the office knew that pussy was my flavor.

Which just made it that much harder to think of a reason to bow out. "Yeah," I said, "fine. Do I need to bring anything?"

"Just your sense of adventure!" she chirped, and fluttered away. I made a face and tossed my hair in silent mockery, then sank back into my office chair. "My sense of adventure and a blindfold," I groaned.

The hen party started at a regular bar, probably because at least half the ladies in attendance needed some liquid courage before they'd ever feel comfortable showing their faces in that kind of establishment. I sipped at whatever fruity thing had been ordered, concealing my distaste with laughter and bawdy jokes. Let everyone else attribute my behavior to being tipsy or to the naughty nature of the party; it was good to be myself for a change.

I was halfway through my first drink and everyone else was tipping away the last of drinks three or four when the maid of honor announced that we would be walking a half block to a "dance bar." She jiggled her tits suggestively, and everyone else hooted and screamed, drawing irritated looks from all over the bar. I turned my smile up a notch, all the while wishing I were invisible.

Our loud, swaying group spilled out onto the sidewalk and catcalled the bride, who was responsible for leading us on our march of what?—shame? naughtiness?—to the strip joint. The guy at the door was a real pro, taking our cover and ushering us to a pair of tables, silently urging with his own calm, quiet demeanor that we lower our energy level a bit. Most of the girls had quieted down, some from apparent shock at the show and others seeming to take his cue. The two or three women—Tara included—who had not stopped shrieking and giggling blended in much more easily with the catcalls of the men around the room and the music that inspired the gyrations of three curvy girls on stage at their stripper poles.

I was somewhat relieved to note that while they were all pretty hot, none of them was especially my type. It would be easier to conceal my appreciation if I weren't also suppressing an urge to drool.

The maid of honor waved until she got someone's attention, and this time the round of drinks was more to my taste. The server brought two huge pitchers of margaritas, and I poured some into a pre-salted glass. The music quieted, prompting hoots of appreciation from around the room. A few of those hoots came from our tables, and I wondered if there were any other closeted lesbians in our ranks.

My amused smile froze on my face as the lights dimmed, the dancers filed toward the end of the stage, and a spotlight lit up a small space in the back. The woman who stepped out was exactly my type.

My mouth went dry and my hand closed on the cold drink. I instinctively took a huge slug, wincing as the tequila burned down my throat, leaving me drier than ever and a little dizzy.

The music started and she slunk onto the stage in a seductive dance, her hips twisting and swirling in lazy figure eights. My clit twinged and I shifted in my seat, wanting to whimper or moan. But that would have been a mistake, because except for the steady beat of the music, the room had fallen dead silent and all eyes were on her.

Like an angel, she drifted across the stage, her eyes sweet and coy while her body screamed sex. Her curves were nothing but woman, but there was something about her that nonetheless whispered to me of something else. It was in the set of her jaw, maybe, or the secrets behind her eyes. In was in her short-trimmed, unvarnished nails and her closely shorn hair, not so unusual in a woman these days, but...together, those things all spoke to me.

My free hand rested in my lap, my nails digging into my

palm as I tried to keep my face relaxed and my gaze nonchalant. She started to peel away the layers of her costume, each one revealing tracts of creamy-smooth skin until—glory be!—she was completely bare but for a tiny thong, her body gyrating with the intensifying music. Men were on their feet near the front of the stage, bills waving in the air, and the lights came up as she stepped forward to accept their tribute. Other dancers filed onto the stage, already pared down to the panties and heels, and took up stations at the poles on either side of my dream boi's center-stage act.

That was when Tara pulled out the wad of ones and dumped them on the table. "I've got a prize for you guys! Everyone who puts a dollar in one of those strippers' thongs gets her name in the hat! Go on! Do it!" She shoved the money toward the center of the table, and a few giggling women snatched up their bills and headed for the stage, their dollars waving in the air like banners.

I felt rooted in place, but Tara hadn't forgotten me, and she seemed determined to "help me out of my shell" as she'd put it earlier in the night. She pushed a small handful of ones into my hand and practically shoved me out of my chair. "Go!"

I stumbled to my feet and headed to the center stage without a conscious decision to do so, my feet carrying me toward the goddess whose worshippers had begun to disperse. She saw me coming and her eyes sparkled as she dropped to her hands and knees and crawled toward the edge of the stage nearest me.

"You're not one of those chicks who comes here on a dare," she said in a throaty murmur, eyes flicking to the hens and back to me.

I folded one dollar and stuffed it in her mouth, leaning forward. "And I know what you are, too," I ventured, my voice sounding bold and confident even as my thudding heart threatened to drown it out. She raised her eyebrows in challenge and I leaned toward her, our shoulders close enough to brush as I tucked the rest of the bills into the side of her thong. "You're a naughty little boi all dressed up like a slut," I whispered for her ears only.

I heard her sharp intake of breath, and as I pulled back, her mouth fell slightly open and the dollar fluttered to the stage. "Yes, Ma'am," she said. I reached to ruffle her hair, my mind's eye seeing how the pixie-like lengths would look gelled into masculine spikes, and backed away. She waited there, kneeling with her eyes downcast, until I'd returned to the table.

Tara was laughing and clapping as the rest of the hens and I returned to the roost. She'd been busy, and scraps of folded white paper littered the table. She scooped them up, mixed them, dumped them and plucked one from the top.

"Megan, you win!" she exclaimed, and from her oversized purse she pulled an oversized rubber cock and handed it straight to me.

Oh, for god's sake!

I glanced past her, back toward the stage, but my naughty little boi in girl's panties was gone. It was probably for the best.

I made a point of not being the first to beg off that night, but I wasn't in the last half, either. I smiled and air-kissed and wished Tara well and promised to call a cab though I'd only had two drinks the entire evening. Outside at last, I took a deep breath of cool, bracing air, ignoring the scents of oil and dust, and tried to remember where I'd parked.

I'd only just turned toward where I thought my car was when I saw a young man lounging against the wall in front of the strip club. His hair came to frosted spikes, he wore a black, studded collar around his neck, and though his figure was hidden beneath a bulky coat, I knew him immediately.

It was the dancing girl. The bad boi who shook his glorious tits at a roomful of strangers at night. My wet dream on two long, long legs.

I froze, startled, and she met my eyes and coyly dropped hers. Then she grinned, and I realized that I was still carrying a fake cock big enough to bludgeon someone with. "Aren't you in enough trouble?" I asked archly, trying to sound stern even though I was sure I was blushing.

"Sorry, Ma'am," she said, immediately contrite. Her voice came from low in her throat, making her sound enough like a guy to pass if you didn't know better. She took a step toward me, but stopped before she got anywhere near close enough to be threatening. "I was actually hoping to catch you. I—how did you know? No one ever knows."

I tipped one shoulder up in a half shrug. "Maybe you just don't attract the right crowd here." I wasn't sure who moved, but the distance between us closed, and without her stripper heels, I was just a hint taller. I brushed my fingers across the tips of her spikes, and then reached down to grip her collar, giving her the gentlest shake. "A good momma always knows when there's a naughty boi in the room. And you've been a very bad boi, haven't you?"

My pulse raced and my lungs constricted like there was a fist around my chest. I could practically feel my eyes dilate, wanting to soak her in, and my cunt...oh god, my cunt was wet.

"Are you going to punish me, then...Momma?" Her almost-masculine tenor had become breathy. Thready. I imagined those adorable nipples pebbled and straining with desire for me. Not what I had expected from some lame hen night out, but well worth the ridiculous posturing.

"Not here," I said, "but if you really deserve a good spanking, then come with me. Momma will take good care of you."

I walked past her, head up and outwardly confident despite the nervous flutter in my stomach, cock clutched in my hand like it was something as innocent as a baguette. The tromp of boots fell in behind me, and I led her to my car. "I'm Megan, by the way, but you can keep calling me Momma. I like it."

"Yes, Momma," she said. I unlocked the car and she slipped into the passenger seat like she belonged as I settled myself behind the wheel. "I'm Cam." A boy's name. It fit her...him.

Neither of us spoke another word as I drove back to my comfortable little house in the suburbs, but my knuckles were white from my grip on the steering wheel, and Cam's hands fluttered like lost birds until he folded them in his lap.

I led him up the walkway to my front door the same way I'd walked him to my car, one step ahead and him following behind, just like a little boy who knew he was about to be punished. My panties were soaked through and we'd barely even touched, and his face was strained with what I could only hope was a similar level of desperate desire.

I hung my coat on the peg by the front door and set my giant dildo on the hall table, reminding myself to come back and retrieve it before anyone could see. Then I folded my arms and turned to Cam, one eyebrow arched. "Well, well," I said, surprising myself with how steady and strong I sounded, "Look what the cat dragged in. Come on, let me see what followed me home."

He obligingly shrugged off the heavy coat, and I saw the flash of uncertainty as he would have just let it drop and realized I'd expected no better. He caught it as it slithered down his arms and hung it beside mine, then stepped back, hands tucked in his back pockets, eyes downcast.

Those beautiful tits filled out the graphic tee in a way the manufacturer had never intended, and his nipples stood straight out as I'd imagined. I wanted to taste their rosy peaks, but I kept a stern look on my face. All things in good time.

Despite the loose jeans he wore, I could see the lump at his crotch, and I stepped forward and grabbed it unceremoniously. He groaned—a high, sweet sound that made my pussy clench.

"What's this?" I asked. But without waiting for an answer, I slid my hand into the front of his pants and pulled the sock from his panties, holding it up in front of him. One side of the sock was damp, and the intoxicating smell of a desperately hot pussy wafted from the fabric as I dangled it in front of his shocked eyes. "Packing?" I shook the sock, inhaling the heady scent as I did. "Who do you think you're fooling, you bad boi?"

"Sorry, Momma," he whispered. His hands fluttered again as if he wanted to reach to take the sock away, and then he stilled them, clasping them at his waist like a schoolgirl.

I brought the sock to my nose for one more deep breath before tossing it aside. "Maybe not yet," I said, "but you will be. You're a very naughty boy, you know."

I tugged the T-shirt up over his head and his beautiful, sweet breasts bounced free. It was more than I could resist, and I gave one perky nipple a savage pinch. He hissed. Whimpered. He was melting into my hands.

"Take off those boots in my house, young man."

"Yes, Momma." The boots fell away, and with a single tug I sent the baggy jeans down to his knees. He stepped out of them and stood before me, tits high and full, with only a pair of white bikini-style panties to hide the wet, drooling mouth of his cunt.

"You like to dance for those men?" I asked him.

He shuffled his feet. "Well, it's easy money."

I pinched his ear, eliciting a yelp that was somewhere between pain, desire, and surprise, and dragged him through my living room to the small guest room/office. My computer hummed in quiet hibernation on my desk in the back corner. My sewing table was neatly organized beside it, and on the wall beside the door, the little twin bed I kept for my few overnight guests awaited us. Guests like my young nephew, whose special Pokémon sheets still lay hidden beneath the white coverlet. I had to suppress the urge to shiver in anticipation.

"Easy money?" I demanded. "Teasing all those nice men? Lying to them? Making them think these tits"—I grabbed a handful of each, kneading them with rough desire as I pushed her back against the wall beside the bed—"make you a sweet little girl? Making them think that they've got a chance at this tight little cunt?" I smacked the cunt in question, eliciting another yelp, higher, louder. Oh, yes.

"I have to pay for school!" he cried.

I returned to his breasts, pinching his nipples hard. His head rocked back, spikes making little crunching sounds as he ground the gelled tips against my clean wall. I used my grip on the tender flesh to pull him forward, spin him around and press him against the wall, his breasts squishing flat beneath our combined pressure as I leaned into him.

"And what sorts of grades do you get?"

"Pretty good. Mostly As and Bs," he gasped. His voice had lost all traces of masculine depth, and my sweet boi panted beneath my onslaught.

"You put on a good show," I said, sliding one hand down the back of his panties. The crotch was soaking wet against my hand, matching my own panties, and there was no resistance as I slid three fingers into his sopping folds and deep into his pussy. "You jiggle those gorgeous tits and smile that innocent smile and you have all those men fooled into seeing what they want to see," I told him, "but I see you for what you are. You're a naughty little boi in women's underpants, and you need to be punished."

He was panting. His nails scraped against my wall as if desperate to hold on to something, and his pussy clenched hard around my fingers, over and over, rhythmic and desperate. I knew this boi. Could read his desires in the lines of his body and the tension thrumming through him, and I knew just what to do next. Without moving my fingers from his desperate cunt, I reached over with the other hand to grasp the coverlet. "It's time for me to do what any good Momma would with a naughty boi like you, and send you to bed." I flipped the coverlet away, revealing the little-boy sheets.

Cam gasped. His pussy tightened so hard around me that I could almost feel my fingers creak, and a tremble started low in his body and moved over him in a wave that I could feel. Then his juices ran soaking over my hand, his pussy spasmed around my fingers and he dropped his head all the way back onto my shoulder as a keening wail of release ripped from his throat.

As his trembling slowed, he dropped his head forward again, and I winced as I heard the clunk of his forehead against the wall. He panted as I withdrew my fingers and took a single step back, but he didn't move for a long moment, hugging the wall, his body half-limp with the afterglow.

Then he turned, eyes wide, and I idly licked his sweet cream from one finger. He was delicious, sweet and tangy, and I hummed in gentle pleasure.

"I've never—no one has—how did you know?" he babbled.

I reached out and slowly wiped his cream across his face, first the back of my hand, and then the front, one cheek, then the other. "I told you," I said, "I see you." Then I turned my back and hitched my shoulders. "Now be a good boi and help Momma with her dress."

His fingers shook as he fumbled the hook and eye open and lowered the zipper slowly down to the small of my back. I shrugged out of the dress and kicked out of my ballet flats, and then reached around, back still toward him, and unlatched my bra. I turned back as it fell away, letting him catch his first sight of my own breasts, smaller than his, but still round and soft. I stepped forward, into his personal space, as I started to hook my panties down.

"I know you're not all bad, my dear boi. So I won't be so cruel as to send you to bed without your supper...this time."

I turned and rolled smoothly onto the bed, my hips just below the small stack of pillows, legs akimbo, my pink lace panties still hooked around one ankle. "Come and eat, sweetheart, Momma's waiting."

With another groan and a whimper of desire, Cam launched himself at the bed, settling himself between my legs to feast at my pussy. He thrust his tongue deep inside my cunt as if he was desperate to lap up every drop, and I cried out at the pleasure and the shock of heat, plucking at my own nipples and caressing the sensitive, flushed skin of my breasts as he fed.

His tongue teased through my slit a few more times, and then he passed with expert grace to my clit, baring the hard little bead with deft strokes of his tongue and licking and sucking it with urgent but careful attention. His fingers slid between my labia, plunging toward my core, and I cried out as the pleasure mounted, quickly bringing me toward my peak.

I was within sight of nirvana when the little brat eased back, gentling his licks, slowing the stroking of his fingers, ignoring the desperate twitching of my hips. He petted his free hand up and down my thigh, quieting the pleasure—banking it. And then, with an expert touch, he brought me up again.

My body, for those moments, was his to control, helpless beneath his lips and hands, a mere instrument for him to strum. And I realized with a shock of pleasure that as clearly as I saw him, he likewise saw into the true heart of my desires. Our merging was a beautiful, perfect blend, and I could feel the harmony of it down to my buzzing, nearly orgasmic core.

So I sat up enough to slap him upside the head, interrupting his careful rhythm for just a moment. "Eat your dinner and quit playing around, you naughty boi!" I cried breathlessly. And with a pleased groan that tingled all the way up to my jaw, he did.

THE WAY

Jove Belle

It's in your smile, the way your mouth curves up on one side in that cheeky, *fuck yes* way that makes me melt, and, once upon a time, made my friend warn me.

"She's trouble," Avi said, but the words rolled off, gathering like a storm at my back.

The first time I met you—fall of freshman year—you smiled oh so properly as you shook hands and worked the room. Then you turned to me and the pretense slipped away. All the politely manufactured polish dropped, replaced by the real you, the devilish spark that said *Just wait until I get you alone.* It was meant for me, but clearly visible to everyone in the room.

"She's a player." Avi pulled my arm until I had no choice but to turn away. In theory, I agreed with him. You'd scanned every girl in the room when you arrived, weighing the pros and cons and cataloguing your conclusions, as if to sample all the options before settling down with the chosen entree of the night. Women were playthings, snacks to be tasted and enjoyed.

But Avi's warning didn't last long. You didn't let it, slipping easily through all his objections with a charming, roguish smile and a wink.

"I'm Jen." You said your name simply, without added fanfare or inflection, and without changing it for a more masculine alternative. Your whole name, I've since learned, Jenna Leone Rampart, could easily lend itself to a more gender-neutral alternative than the unmistakably feminine Jen. I asked you once why you didn't go by Lee or possibly Ram. They seem better fits for the short, almost shaved hair and the button-down men's dress shirts you prefer. You laughed and said, "That's not who I am." So comfortable then and now with who you are.

"Rosa." I forgot to shake your hand, too caught up in your smile to think about anything else. It was enough that I was able to find my voice, remember my name. Anything else was impossible. You reached down, took my hand in yours and shook it gently, gentlemanly.

"Rosa." You said my name with much more care and consideration than your own. You caressed the letters, speaking so softly, so reverently, I was certain that my name, heretofore unknown to me, held the answers to all of life's more difficult questions. I wanted to taste it the way you did, feel it with the same depth. It'd been mine all along, yet I had no idea it was a treasure until you showed me.

It's in your eyes, in the way you wink and drape my hand over your arm, assigning yourself to be my old-fashioned charming escort of the evening. You covered my hand with yours and my reservations melted even further. Player? Maybe you were before that night, but the carefully collated collection of women was lost, left behind to never be revisited after you took my hand for the first time.

"Rosa?" Avi followed us through the party, concerned for my loss of reputation if you lived up to yours. Clearly, his tone said, I'd lost my mind and couldn't be trusted alone. My clothes would fall off at any moment without him there to stand between me and a night of debauchery. He looked at you with clear disdain, untrusting, wary. His opinion of you has changed over the years, but that night he worked hard to keep us apart. "Shouldn't we be going? You have that early test tomorrow."

It was a lie, a prearranged signal between friends designed to keep us both safe from the predators that trolled campus parties. We'd used it so many times before and each time I'd been over-whelmed with gratitude at his clear insight, his ability to see danger where it wasn't always obvious. He'd rescued me when a "nice" girl slipped her hand up my skirt without permission, when another slipped her not-so-nice drugs into my drink and when yet another pinned me to the wall, blocking others from seeing my struggle to escape. Those were the dangers of being small, of being cute, of being feminine. It was amazing we still went to parties, but for every bad encounter, there were ten other women who understood that a night out didn't have to end in sex. Besides, with Avi at my side, why should I worry?

I blinked a few times, clearing my vision and tearing my gaze away from you. "No, Avi, I think you're mistaken. I don't have any tests until next week."

That wouldn't be enough to convince him to leave us alone completely, but at least it signaled that I was happy with the progression of things, that I had no desire to end the evening so quickly. Avi blustered, unsure where to go now that I'd changed course and left him without a map.

Instead of Avi, you responded, "Are you sure? I don't want to be the reason you fail a test."

The look of surprise on Avi's face was worth all the sulking and scowling he'd done in the past thirty minutes since you'd arrived. You couldn't be truly nice, his expression clearly said, you were only out for one thing. At that point, I didn't care if you were. I'd willingly let you slip your hand as high up my skirt as you wanted.

"I'm positive. I'm all yours."

It's the way you walk, your swagger more pronounced, more evident when I'm with you than when you're alone. You squared your shoulders, held your head high and simply owned that room, owned the world. That night was the first time Avi left a party before me, turning responsibility for my care, my safety over to you.

"Ro, I'm beat. I'm going to head back." The party had been a bust for him, filled wall to wall with beautiful, butch bois for me to savor, but not a single gay boy in the mix for him to play with. I was surprised he lasted as long as he did.

You shook his hand and punched him in the arm. All the while, you kept your other arm wrapped tight around my waist, your fingers working a steady rhythm against the fabric of my dress, stretching, pulling, searching. The look on your face, so smug, yet unguarded and bewildered. I'd chosen to stay with you instead of retreating with Avi, the friend I'd arrived with, the friend who'd stayed with me despite your best efforts to ditch him. The swagger, after that, was more pronounced than ever, telecasting your victory with every step. I felt like a beautiful prize.

No more than ten minutes after Avi left, you guided me into the night. The temperature, drastically colder now that the sun had set, caught me off guard. Fall had firmly arrived, no more dance between seasons. You held me close, your arm a blanket around my shoulders, and walked faster. You didn't ask which direction, and I didn't argue when you passed my street and kept traveling south toward campus.

When we arrived at your door, a single dorm versus the two-bedroom apartment I shared with Avi off campus, you paused with your hand on the knob and asked, "Is this okay?"

It's the way you touch my face, your fingers soft and gentle, yet so very eager. That night, you traced the surface of my skin, cataloguing the contours over and over, memorizing them until they replaced the faces of the other women you'd been with before that night. You were slow, careful, and I closed my eyes to feel the joy of "Yes, yes, yes." The movement stopped, your fingers light against my lips.

"Rosa?" I opened my eyes, expecting to find the world changed, melted down and rebuilt from the inside to match the transformation I felt with every stroke of your fingers. My breath caught in my throat and I couldn't find even the simplest words to respond.

You asked again, "Is this okay?"

I nodded, the movement slow to start, jerky, and then urgent, out of control. It was so much more than okay and everything inside me screamed at my mouth to work, at my tongue to form words. Nothing came except for the low, gut-deep moan as you took my mouth in a kiss.

It's in your kiss, the way your lips explore, taking what you want and giving back liberally as your tongue slips inside, hot and demanding. "You're mine," it said as you stroked into me, tasting in a way that promised so much more than just a fleeting exchange in a darkened doorway. You clung to me, clutching my shoulders to pull me so close that your heaving chest forced the air from my lungs.

When we parted, with a gasp and whimper, the question of okay or not was gone from your face, replaced with a promise to own every last part of me. In the years since then, you've kissed me many times, each time taking my heart with every careful, demanding, heated brush of your mouth, every lick of your tongue as you prize my lips apart to climb inside and know me from the inside out. And every time, I open myself to you, pleading with you to take, take, take.

"Inside?" I sounded as desperate as I felt, my brain, my thoughts melted from the heat building inside me, swarming upward and threatening to engulf us both, threatening to burn down the building around us.

"God, yes." And for the first time, you fumbled, your movements rushed, clumsy. The key slipped from your hand, hitting the carpet and bouncing a few feet. It came to a stop against the wall, slanted on its side. You looked despondent, your gaze flitting between the dropped key and my mouth, my lips parted in anticipation. "Fuck it."

You abandoned the key, wrapping one hand around my head, twisting your fingers in my hair and pulling my face to yours. The kiss was open, sloppy, wet, and I couldn't get close enough, clutching your lapels in my hands and holding tight enough to make my knuckles white. You wrapped your other arm around my waist, holding me to you, making me feel you everywhere as the heat of our bodies flowed like lava through me.

A sharp bang on the wall next to us, followed by drunken laughter and the loss of your lips from mine. I searched for you, chasing after you with a moan, too dazed to understand what happened.

"Take it inside." A house of a man clapped you on the back, his friends laughing and cheering. He pushed his way between us, inserted the lost key into the lock, and twisted the knob. I should have thanked him for providing us with some privacy, but I was beyond caring. You could have done whatever you wanted to me, wherever you wanted to do it.

It's in the drop of your head, the embarrassed flush of your skin when you know you've been caught and can't quite bring yourself to care. It's happened too many times, you with your hands on me, your tongue inside me, and me too disoriented to be embarrassed. That first night, you shuffled your weight from foot to foot, your face tinged red with uncertainty, and the suave, seductive mystique shattered. Suddenly I could breathe again.

I laughed with your friends and your face turned even redder, but I couldn't stop. The flow of breath, the release of tension, the giddy wave of hormones on top of the heavy flood of phero-mones and I was drunk on the moment, reveling in the closeness of you and what it meant, what it might mean for the future. It was too soon, but I was hopeful, buoyed by the inexplicable, irrefutable, inextricable connection flowing between us. Even with your friends there, the darkness of our alcove exposed and vulnerable, you still sought me out, your arm working tighter around my waist with every moment, your fingers bunching the fabric of my dress, pulling and searching for me.

"Thanks, Carter." You snatched the key from his outstretched fingers, squeezing it tight in your palm and not giving it a chance to fall from your grip again. The laughter continued as you guided me inside, your mouth so close to my ear your heavy want washed over my skin and shivered through my body with each exhale. You didn't look at your friends again as you smoothly closed the door and pushed me against it, your body so tight, so hot against mine, I worried the flat wooden surface would give way with the heat.

The laughter, like steam released from a kettle, evaporated as you looked into my eyes. Yearning, deep and soulful, gripped me viscerally, twisting from you to me until my insides were knotted and the only thing that mattered in that moment was the promise of more. Perfect, inexplicable, and so fragile because we both knew it was once in a lifetime and our only options were to seize it, and each other, or to let it pass.

It's in the curve of your arm, the strength in your tight, sinewy muscles as you hold me to you like I might evaporate before your eyes. I've never grown tired of the security I feel when you hold me, like I'm china, precious, rare and worthy of extreme care. That night, as I felt your arms around me for the first time, felt the strain as you battled between pulling me closer and holding back because you didn't want to crush me, I knew I'd never find that kind of peace and clarity with anyone else.

"Do you feel it?" You rested your forehead against mine, your mouth so close I could feel your breath, feel your lips as you spoke, but too far away because I wanted to kiss you again, not talk. "You do, right? It's not just me. I'm not imagining it."

You were so vulnerable, so raw, all your swagger stripped away leaving you and your genuine show of emotion. I had no choice but to lay myself bare before you. Otherwise I would have been unworthy. I wouldn't have deserved the feeling of being cherished that you were offering so freely.

I nodded, my gaze locked on yours, open and unguarded. In that moment I had no secrets, no hope of recovery if you decided to pull back, to protect your vulnerable heart. And it terrified me. Yet there you were, offering yourself. God, I wanted to partake.

"Yeah," I whispered, "I feel it. Right here."

I guided your hand to rest on my chest so you could feel the pounding of my heart, so hard and so fast I was afraid of what it meant. You flattened your palm, the outside edges of your thumb and pinkie cresting the sides of my breasts and giving me another reason for my heart to race. You closed your eyes and we stayed there, with you feeling me, feeling us, for several long moments, long enough for me to lose track of everything except for the feel of your arm holding me close and the burn of your palm against my chest.

It's the way you cup my face, curving your palm around my jaw and brushing your thumb in an endless arc over my cheek. You kissed me again, slower this time, gentle, exploring, savoring. I tilted my head back, letting it rest against the door and opening myself fully to you. I didn't fight for the power, overwhelmed and swept away by the tide of you rolling your tongue against mine. You caressed...massaged...owned, calling a moan from deep inside me, low and guttural and completely beyond my control.

Before I realized the loss of your hand on my face, I felt your fingers inching the fabric of my dress up until they could tickle against the over-sensitized flesh of my inner thigh. I gasped, shocked when you brushed high enough to feel the fabric of my panties, feel the heat and wet through the thin, inconsequential cotton.

I hadn't dressed for sex, taking care with the outer layer, but not bothering with fancy undergarments. The front of my panties said "Saturday." It was Thursday. Nothing about them said sexy.

My legs slid apart and I muttered, "Thank you." To myself, to you, I didn't know. I hadn't willfully opened my legs, so the moment your fingers slipped beneath the elastic edge of my panties and slid through the moist heat of my sex was owing to complete divinity.

"God, you're perfect," you said huskily, your voice strained. Urgent. Needy.

You stayed there forever, just rolling your fingers through my folds, drawing my desire to a sharp point without ever pushing me over. My legs trembled, my heart thundered, and all I could do was beg. "Please. More. God." Over and over in an unending circle as I clutched your shoulder hard enough to carve little moons into your flesh through your shirt.

You stared at me, rapt. I chased your hand, urging you to unfurl your fingers, to plunge them inside, to focus tight circles on my clit, something, anything. Yet you kept up the maddening buildup, drawing me out, extending my pleasure until I was wrung out, too weak, too shaky to hold myself up. You strengthened your hold on me, the flex and bulge of your bicep registering peripherally, serving to turn me on even more.

"I've got you."

You dropped your mouth to my throat, licking, sucking, and I was lost in an exquisite haze, helpless and dependent upon you to guide me home, something that wouldn't happen until you were ready.

"I want to be inside of you, I want to feel your walls clench and grab as I fuck you through orgasm after orgasm." As you spoke, you slid one finger inside me and held it there. I gasped, whimpered and pleaded with you to finish me. You smiled into my neck, the curve of your mouth pulling at my flesh. "I want to pin you to the bed and watch as you take my cock. I want you facedown with me behind you. I want you on top of me, riding until we both pop. I want you on your knees with my cock in your mouth. I want all of you."

Your words, dirty, salacious and so fucking sexy, worked deeper inside me than the one finger that was probing, but not stroking. I was at critical mass, ready to explode with the slightest breath, the barest twitch of your nail against my clit, and still you held me there.

"Tonight, however, all I want is you. Against this wall, with my hand in your panties, teasing until you overflow and drown me in come."

It's in your touch, the way that you know exactly what to do, exactly what to say. The way you can drag it out until I'm ready to throw myself from a cliff. Or you can drive me from unsuspecting to exploding orgasm before I'm fully aware that I'm on my back with you above me. That night, with your finger inside me, your breath on my skin and my heart meeting yours for the first time, you brought me to a place I'd never experienced before. A place where I was loved, cherished and completely, entirely desired.

"Do you want that?" you asked as you pulled your finger out in one long smooth stroke and I cried out. You had to give me more. You'd promised. I would die, slowly, painfully and excruciatingly turned on beyond return if you didn't. "Do you?"

You nipped at my throat, the sting of teeth sharp and immediate, grounding me in the moment like nothing before. I'd been on the verge of floating away, and you pulled me back to you. "Yes, yes, yes, yes." I gasped out the answer, unable to stop at just one word. I needed you to hear me, to know how much I needed.

And then you gave me...everything. With your sure stroke against my clit, circling hard and fast and so certain, I came apart. I didn't orgasm, not like every other experience I'd had with it, at least. This was complete, starting in my cunt and rolling out until my whole body was engulfed in a wave of clench and release, flying and destined to crash. No one can ride that high forever. You eased me, caressing me and bringing me down, setting my feet on solid ground and holding me up instead of letting me fall.

I slumped, weak and wholly spent, in your arms, and you guided me to your bed. That first night, I fell asleep in your arms, satisfied and rummy from sex in a way I'd never felt before. I've slept in your bed every night since, and you've kept every dirty promise you whispered to me as you brought me to orgasm against your dorm room door.

It's in your smile, your eyes and the tight swagger of your hips.

It's your touch on my face, your kiss on my mouth and the drop of your head that says you're caught, but not sorry.

It's the curve of your arm around my waist, and the way you cup my face.

It's in your touch.

RESURRECTION

Victoria Villasenor

I sat at the table, the smell of coffee floating around me, quiet chatter and the clatter of plates and glasses drifting through the cafe. This was my favorite Sunday morning routine: sitting in front of a huge window, the sunlight streaming in and warming my back as I watched people heading down to the beach and the shopkeepers getting their stores ready for another day of sea air and tourists.

Today, though, I was restless. I needed something specific, but I didn't feel like doing the bar crawl to find it. I wanted a sweet tongue to use all day and night, a warm back to drag my nails over. And I have these things at home, but a few times a year I want something other than the beautiful femme who warms my bed and heart. Today I wanted a boi, a cute one to make scream in the way only a butch can. I sighed and stared out the window, my clit aching and swollen. I squinted as a reflection appeared in the glass. Like something out of my dreams, a young butch strutted into the coffee house, her low-riding jeans hugging slim hips that showed the top of her Calvin Klein boxers. I turned in my seat to appraise her.

Her hair was short and thick with a long piece falling over her eyes. She flicked it back, revealing startling blue eyes. She was shorter than I am, but not by much. Her breasts, assuming they weren't bound, were small and high. Perfect.

My clit twitched again and this time got even harder, pressing against the seam of my jeans and making me hot. I tilted my head and continued to stare as she ordered, her lightly muscled arms flexing as she leaned on the counter, flirting with the femme serving her. I grinned. Exactly what I needed.

She got her coffee and moved to another plush chair by the window, facing me. I sipped my coffee, thinking of all the things I could do to that young, supple body. When I began to picture her writhing under the sting of my belt, I couldn't stand it anymore.

I moved to stand quietly next to her, my arms folded. When she looked up, I squatted down next to her and looked directly into her eyes. "I'd like you to come home with me. Right now."

She blinked and then laughed lightly. "You're not really my type, buddy."

"And you're not really mine. Except for right at this moment."

I watched her mind work as she took me in: my short black hair, my thickly muscled arms covered in tats, the plain leather bracelet on my wrist. I am bigger, stronger, slightly older. And I knew that she could feel the sex oozing from my skin as my clit continued its wild contractions against the seam of my Levi's.

"I don't..." she said quietly, but trailed off when I stood and offered my hand. She stared at it for a long moment and then brushed it away with her own. Standing abruptly she pushed passt me and strode out the door, her back stiff as she clearly tried to appear unfazed.

I followed. Once outside I grabbed the back of her neck and led her to my truck, opened the door for her and pushed her roughly inside, letting my hand graze the side of her chest. No binding. Those small tits were just perfect.

I watched her swallow convulsively, her hands clenched tightly and her jaw working in rhythm to her pulse. She wasn't going to bottom for me easily, this one, although she clearly wanted to. I could tell by how tightly she was clenching her thighs together—so tightly they were shaking.

I got in, leaned over, squeezed her throat and kissed her roughly. She stayed stiff, but opened her mouth to let me in.

"Good boi," I whispered, and felt her stiffen even further.

"I'm not a goddamn boi," she said through gritted teeth.

"You are today."

We didn't say another word until we pulled into my driveway. The house is set far back from the street, and tall old trees line every side, making it private and somewhat ominous looking.

I turned to face her, and saw that she'd gone slightly pale and was holding onto the sides of the seat with white knuckles. "What's your safeword?"

"I don't have one. I haven't... I mean, I've never..."

She swallowed hard and continued to stare straight ahead of her.

"How about berry? That's something you won't scream randomly." I was only half kidding, trying to get her to relax slightly. If she didn't relax, it would take far too long to get her where I wanted her. And I wanted her bad.

"Why?" she asked.

"Why, what?" I was so distracted by thoughts of her naked that her question lost me.

"Why me. Why a butch?"

I tilted my head and considered her question. With a sigh, I nodded toward the house. "C'mon. We'll talk inside. And if you really don't want to go for it, I'll take you back to the coffee house, no problem. Okay?"

She visibly relaxed and nodded.

I should've done the fucking bar crawl. It would have been

easier. Now I had to have a philosophical conversation about why I wanted to drive my cock inside this luscious butch and listen to her give it up.

Inside, I tossed her a bottle of water from the fridge and opened one myself. Leaning against the kitchen counter, I watched as she wandered the living room, looking at photographs and running her fingers across the furniture. She stopped in front of a picture of me and my girl and shot me a quizzical look.

"She's at our other place. I use this one when I'm working in the local office."

"Does she know?"

"She does. It's not often, but she gets it."

I watched as she tried to process that. "Come here."

She moved toward me, and I could see her uncertainty in every step. It fueled the fire between my legs. Pushing a butch's boundaries, making her question and falter, is a heady feeling. I pulled her quickly toward me, turning her so her back was against my chest.

I nuzzled her neck, letting my large, calloused hands wander over her soft cotton T-shirt. "We're so strong, aren't we? Us butches. They lean on us, they depend on us, they listen to what we say. Sometimes, though..." I reached under her shirt and pinched her nipples. "Don't you want to let go? Don't you want to be the one taking it, lying back and letting someone else take the reins? Don't you want to be able to beg for it, to let go and not have to control anything at all? To just enjoy a good fuck without worrying that you'll look weak?" I felt her pulse beating rapidly under my lips as I kissed her neck and knew I would get what I wanted when her ass pressed against the seven-inch cock I was strapping. "Sometimes, don't you want to be filled, to be done, to scream it all out and not have to be strong? Don't you want to be the one riding that silver wave of pain, losing yourself in the endorphins and submission?"

She whimpered as my fingertips closed tightly on her nipples, pulling and twisting. She ground against my cock and whispered, "Have you? Have you done this?"

I pulled her hips hard against me, bending her forward and making small circles against her tight ass.

"I have. I've knelt in front of a butch and sucked her cock, just like you're going to. I've done what she's told me to, and I've let her fuck me just the way I fuck my femme. I've given her all of my control, and let myself come and hurt and scream for it."

She moaned and pushed harder against me. Her skin was warm, flushed, and her voice was husky with need. Yes, she wanted this. And I was ready to give it to her. I let go of her hips and she stumbled forward, off balance. I grabbed the back of her neck, lifted her to her feet, and dragged her to the bedroom. I let her get a look at the room, with its open toy cupboard filled with all sorts of leather gear, and the bed with its heavy iron rings on the headboard and posts, before I shoved her facedown on the bed and held her there.

"Tell me you want it. Tell me you want my cock in your tight butch pussy."

She shook her head and I squeezed harder, pushing my thigh between her legs.

"Say it. Tell me you want me to fuck you, to let you lose control."

"I've never had a cock," she whispered, her eyes tightly shut. I could hear the fear in her voice and I knew what it cost her to admit it.

Goddamn. A virgin butch. I swallowed hard and tried to control the waves of lust swamping me. I wanted her, and I was going to have her. But she'd have to be dripping wet for me to get my seven inches inside her, since I didn't have anything smaller in the house.

"Then let's fix that, shall we?" I pulled her up, then pushed her to her knees. "What's your safeword?" I asked, unbuttoning my jeans slowly, stroking the length of my cock as she watched, transfixed.

"Berry."

"Do you understand when to use it? That it's when you really can't take any more, or really don't like whatever I'm doing?"

She nodded and flicked an irritated glance up at me. "I know what a goddamn safeword is. It's not like this makes me some kind of fucking untried femme."

I threw my head back and laughed, and grabbed her by the back of her neck to shove her face against my crotch. "Okay, okay." I took the cock out of my jeans and slid the tip over her lips. I could feel her reluctance, her head straining against my hand.

"Show me what you like your femme to do. Show me how you like your cock sucked, baby."

That's all it took. She opened wide and took it in, sucking it like a pro, her cheeks pulling as she sucked hard and long in deep strokes. I moaned and eased my grip on her head as she sucked me off. I watched as the flesh-colored cock slipped in and out of her rosy red mouth, her pink tongue circling it, licking it, her hand holding the base hard against my clit. Before she could make me come I pulled her head back, making her stop.

I caught my breath for a moment and let her catch hers too. I could see the uncertainty still lingering in her eyes, the sudden realization of what she was doing beginning to overwhelm her. Before it could take over, I pulled her to her feet and bent her over the bed. I made quick work of her jeans, pulling the black leather belt from them and grinning as goose bumps appeared across her skin at the sound. She kicked off her boots and I yanked her jeans from her legs, keeping her moving to keep her from thinking. I threw her black CK boxers to the floor and nearly fainted at the smell of her arousal.

I knew what she was feeling. My first time under another

butch I fought like a demon. I wouldn't give up the control I'd fought so hard to keep in place, but once I started coming under her relentless tongue, I knew she had given me a gift. Even butches need emotional and psychological release. And sometimes we can get it easier from a butch who understands that, than from a femme who might see it as weakness. I was going to show this hot young butch what it meant to let go. I palmed her dripping wet pussy and felt her tense. Slowly, gently I began teasing her clit until she relaxed under the palm I held against the middle of her back.

Her juices filled my hand and she began to writhe against my palm. But I wanted her wet, not coming. Not yet.

"Tie me down."

"Oh no, little butch. You're going to give this up freely, not because I make you."

She groaned into the bedcover as I slid a finger inside her. God she was tight. For a moment I worried about hurting her, but when she suddenly arched and came hard in my hand, all thought left my mind.

I pushed her onto the bed. "Undress."

Without a word she pulled off her shirt and sports bra. But she wouldn't make eye contact, not after coming in another butch's palm. I stripped off my clothes, leaving on my black sports bra and boxers, my thick cock hanging out the front, ready to plow into her. I watched as her eyes slid over my body and then looked away, her jaw working again in obvious fear and confusion.

"Lie back."

She did, but her body was tense again. With an internal sigh, I slid down between her legs. At the first touch of my tongue I knew she would want to bolt, so I hooked my arms under her slim, tight thighs and held her to my face.

Butch or femme, andro or tweener, this one spot we all have

in common. And while us butches might not let our lovers play with it very much, god it feels so good when it happens. She cried out and pushed against my face as my tongue slid over her large, pulsing clit. Her hands wrapped in the sheets and she pulled at them frantically. I stroked her until I felt her body tense with lust instead of fear and then really began to suck her off, taking her clit between my teeth, licking it, biting it, drawing it deep into my mouth. Her low-throated moans turned to curses as I kept stopping just before she could come. Suddenly I stopped and moved on top of her. Getting a gentle but strong hold on her wrists and pinning them above her head I whispered, "Breathe," and then pushed my cock into her in one long, deep thrust. I felt the brief barrier give way as she shouted and strained against my hold on her.

I waited until she opened her eyes again and then began a slow, deep rhythm, the oldest one in creation. Well, with a bit of imagination thrown in, anyway.

She relaxed and began moving against me, under me, and I let go of her wrists. She raised her knees and I groaned as I went even deeper inside her, listening to her wetness mix with mine as I began to truly fuck her. There is nothing like a tight butch pussy riding a thick butch cock. The thought alone nearly shoved me over the edge, but I wanted more.

When I pulled out she gasped and tensed again. Her eyes were glassy and she looked high. I knew the feeling, and I knew she was about to get much higher.

"On your stomach."

She tensed again and began to shake her head.

I grabbed her ankles in my hands and twisted, forcing her onto her stomach. In the blink of an eye I had her arms behind her back, and had wrapped bondage tape around her wrists.

"You wanted to be tied, little boi? You've got what you want. Now it's my turn."

I picked up the belt I'd taken off her pants, wrapped it around my hand and lightly slapped her thighs with it. I grinned as she jumped at the contact and then began whipping her with it in earnest, from the dip of her knees to her lower back. Each strike turned her beautiful pale skin sunset pink and made me hotter and hotter. When her yells turned to moans and then to soft whimpers as I struck harder and harder, I knew she was high enough. I knelt on the bed behind her and pulled her up by her hips. Spreading her asscheeks I poured lube into her asscrack, smearing it liberally in and around her tiny little hole. She began to struggle for real now, trying to shimmy away from me on the bed.

"Oh no, sweet boi. You want this. Do you think I can't see you dripping for it? You'll like this, baby boi. Just relax. Or don't. I'll like it either way."

I chuckled cruelly for effect, thinking the whole time how hot she was and how I wanted her to remember this for a long time to come. I slid one finger into her ass and groaned in response to her scream. She was driving me over the edge, and I was going to need to come soon. I fucked her slow and deep with one finger before adding another. She cried out, but pushed back onto my fingers. Oh god. I added a third finger and drove into her relentlessly. Her cries turned into pleas and I twisted and turned, fucked and rammed her sweet, tight ass, watching as her hips slammed back to match my movements. I felt her orgasm building and knew it was time. With no warning I slid four fingers into her swollen wet pussy and continued fucking her ass.

She screamed, threw herself back onto me, and with a hoarse cry she came, her cream squirting all over my hand, her ass and her pussy spasming around my fingers. Her body jerked and arched, and the pillowcase was torn and crumpled in her fists.

We came down together slowly. I gently and carefully pulled

out and then rolled her onto her side to give her a break. I went to the bathroom and washed her cream from my hands. I took off my cock and threw it in the tub. While I would gladly ride a femme for another hour, until she begged me to stop, this sweet butch's pussy couldn't take it again. She stared at me through vacant, glassy eyes when I came back into the room. I wondered if she had any idea how beautiful she looked. A sweet, lithe young butch, bound, fucked, beaten and satiated. It is good to be reminded sometimes that we still have a soft side. I'd just reminded this one very, very well. Now it was her turn to remind me.

"My turn."

She moaned as I pulled her to a sitting position. I let her catch her breath before moving her onto the floor, to her knees.

"Make me come. Make me come and I'll make you so high you'll take weeks to come down," I said.

I pulled off my boxers and moved to her face. God yes. There's so much power in having a butch on her knees, sucking me off. I closed my eyes and let my head drop back. I rested my hands on her head as she began to lick me, timidly at first and then with growing confidence as I made the noises she was used to getting from any woman. She licked and sucked at my clit like an old pro. Her teeth grazed it and then bit down on it, and that was all it took. I held her face tightly against my pussy and came hard, riding her mouth for all it was worth until every last bit was gone.

I sagged against the bed, still holding her head in my hands.

Staring down at her, I could see the surprise and realization in her eyes. It felt good to make another butch come. It was powerful to make another butch lose control and give it up. Gathering the last of my energy I picked her up, threw her facedown on the bed again, and ripped off the bondage tape. I yanked her up by her short hair, pressed her to the bedpost and tied her hands to the thick ring at the top. She was stretched beautifully, her rippled muscles outlined against the hard wood.

I gently touched the three areas of her back I was about to use, and then I began. The flogger slapped each section in turn... shoulder blades, middle back, lower back. Shoulder blades, middle back, lower back.

Over and over again, harder and harder, until I was putting my back into the swings and she was writhing and shouting, her back arching to meet every stinging stroke. When her back was a beautiful crisscross of red welts and stripes, some opening slightly to reveal tiny droplets of blood, I dropped the whip and pressed my body against hers. She screamed at the sudden pressure but relaxed quickly against me. Reaching between her legs I pushed two fingers into her tightly swollen pussy and fucked her, slow and gentle, deep and firm. I took her, made her let go in that instant, and as she came hard against my hand, her arms straining against the bedpost, I felt the last vestige of her control leave.

She rode my hand for an eternity, her orgasm coming in sweeping, intense waves. I rode them with her, my face pressed to the hot welts on her back, my other arm draped tightly around her waist, holding her to me, grounding her. When she finished, spent, tears rolled slowly down her face. I knew those tears. They're the tears of relief, of release, of resurrection. They are the tears that come when you have let go so completely, and you're still safe, still you.

Without letting go of her waist, I released her wrists and half carried her to the bed. Pulling the covers down I slid in next to her and covered us both. I spooned her and felt the rhythm of her heart as it slowed to a normal pace. I was almost drifting off when she suddenly flipped to face me. Roughly she shoved my thighs apart.

"Sorry," she said, and thrust three fingers into my still wet pussy.

I groaned as she built up a strong rhythm, her long fingers touching just the right places. Suddenly she added another finger, and then another, and suddenly the little boi butch was fisting me. I screamed, my already low voice coming out in a feral roar. Her fist disappeared inside me, only to be pulled almost all the way out before being slammed back in. I rode it hard, and as I was about to come her other hand closed around my throat. I came hard, bucking against her fist, her water-blue eyes never leaving mine. My come covered her fist and I moaned out the last of it before collapsing back onto the bed, totally spent.

She pulled out slowly and grinned at the wetness dripping from her hand and arm.

"Bathroom's over there." I nodded in the right direction and closed my eyes. We still had the whole night ahead of us, and I had a cupboard full of toys. I was ready, and I had a feeling she was too.

CRICKET

Anna Watson

What a funny little woman," said my coworker.

I looked up from my computer to see our ten o'clock in the parking lot, a client I hadn't met before. She was getting out of an old, dark-blue Chevy Impala, a real granddad car. She opened the back door, took out a small leather briefcase, then checked twice that the doors were locked before making her way over to our law office. Her movements were precise and purposeful and she held herself stiffly upright, carrying the briefcase almost reverently. As she reached the door, Arvid, the senior partner, came rushing out to greet her, ushering her quickly into his inner sanctum with just a quick command of, "Coffee!" over his shoulder.

I knocked and brought in the tray. Arvid introduced me to Heloise Taylor, saying that her mother had died suddenly and that they were discussing the will. I murmured my sympathies as I set out the coffee things.

Heloise was sitting on the Hard Chair. I hate that chair, and have gone so far as to haul it out to the curb on trash day, but

Arvid always brings it back in. He says some people need a hard chair, and it did seem to particularly suit Heloise. Arvid is actually a pretty good lawyer. His hearty uncle act can be very effective, but I wasn't sure he was clicking with Heloise. He must not have been sure, either, because he invited me to stay.

Heloise was the sole survivor, the last of her family. She and her mother had lived together, and it was obvious that Heloise was in shock at her mother's death. Still, she was completely present at the table, paying close attention to everything Arvid was saying. It was almost as if, even in the depths of her grief—especially in the depths of her grief—she wanted to show us how well she was caring for her mother.

The will had a few minor complications, nothing serious, but Heloise did have to come in several times after that first appointment. She always came alone. I always sat in. I wished there had been someone we could call to help her, a niece or a cousin, but she kept saying that there was no one and that she was fine. The last time she came in, she waited until Arvid had left the room, and then stood to shake my hand.

"Thank you for your help, Tiffany. I appreciate everything you've done for me."

I watched out the window as she made her way to her car. She was wearing the same clothes she'd worn for the first appointment, when my coworker had called her a funny little woman. I wondered if they had been her mother's clothes, or something her mother chose for her: beige polyester elastic-waisted slacks in a large check, circa 1975, a turquoise sweater set, black lace-up old-lady shoes with white athletic anklets. I could see what was so amusing, of course, but Heloise had her own dignity. And it was her dignity that I had been noticing. And another thing. I was pretty sure that her short graying hair had been cut by a barber.

After Heloise stopped coming into the office, I looked for her in town. I just found myself thinking about her, keeping an eye out, wondering how she was doing. Once I thought I saw her at Albertson's in the frozen food department and another time when I was getting a pain au chocolat at Le Petit Outre, but I was mistaken. The last place I expected to run into her was Miller's.

Miller's is Missoula's only independently owned department store, now in serious decline. It's fabulous in there. They have a beautiful line of slips, as well as goodies from the past like dress shields, shoulder pads and outdated foundation garments. This particular late afternoon, the lingerie department was completely deserted, as was often the case. I was dreamily perusing the wall of panties when I felt someone beside me, and, turning brusquely, almost knocked into Heloise.

"Heloise!" I cleared my throat. "So nice to see you! How are you doing?"

"I ran out of dainties," she blurted out. "I mean underwear. Um, drawers."

"Well, you came to the right place," I said, raising an eyebrow.

She began to blush. It was the most beautiful thing. Her cheeks flushed, her ears began to take on color, and her neck and chest—the little bit of it I could see above her buttoned-up blouse—turned a solid, brick red. I couldn't take my eyes off her.

"Mother called them dainties," Heloise began to explain, stammering with embarrassment. "She had words for every-thing. And she's the one who shopped for them. I shovel and keep the car tuned up, and she shopped for dainties. I just came here to see, if I could find..." she stopped, looking at me helplessly.

After that chance meeting, when I helped her choose some plain, white underwear, I heard from Heloise regularly. The first time, she called me at the office to see if we could use some elk meat a neighbor had given her in exchange for keeping their plants watered when they were on vacation. Arvid, still fuming because he'd been unable to bag an elk this year himself, accepted the gift with slightly bad grace. Heloise began calling my personal line, and then my cell, with offers of other small gifts: would I allow her to take my car to be inspected, as she'd noticed my sticker was about to expire and she was sure I was extremely busy; she knew where to get some cheap firewood if I had a fireplace or a woodstove; she was free during the day if I needed any other errands run—maybe I had a dog at home who would enjoy a walk at noon?

"Are you working, Heloise?" I asked her once, and she said no, that her father had provided for her and her mother. That after high school she thought she might like to work for a vet, but it never panned out. "That was when Daddy was sick," she said. "And Mother needed me at home. She needed me after he died, too. And Daddy asked me to take care of her. I did. I took good care of her."

I began to depend on her help for things a lady alone such as myself can easily find herself ignoring, little repair jobs around the house, car maintenance. I was certainly happy to have her walk Medusa, the Bergamasco my ex had insisted on when we'd moved to Missoula and I had inherited when she fled. Dusa and Heloise adored each other.

One Saturday, Heloise called to ask, very hesitantly, for a favor from me. She wondered if I would go shopping with her for new clothes. She would very much appreciate my help.

We went to Miller's of course, and had been there for only a few minutes, going quickly through racks of blouses and skirts, when she touched my arm. She was wired, kind of in overdrive, almost silly.

"Do you think it would be all right if we looked there?" She was gesturing to the men's department.

"Of course!" My heart rate speeded up as we walked over, and I thought about how fine she would look in a pair of jeans, a western shirt and cowboy boots. She went right to the polo shirts and khakis, though, and started trying to figure out her size. I helped, keeping an eye out for the elderly queen who worked there, just to make sure he wouldn't bother Heloise or ask awkward questions. He usually spent a lot of time meticulously folding the scarves and ascots, but he wasn't there. It was early evening, a time when most of the staff seemed to go on break.

By now, Heloise had a pile of clothes in her arms, and we were both giggling, brushing up against each other accidentally-on-purpose. I took her to the dressing rooms in lingerie. No one else was down there.

"The one at the end is big enough for both of us," I told her, leading the way into the dimly lit warren of cubicles. The dressing rooms were as old-fashioned as the rest of the store, with solid doors, scuffed wooden floors, pincushions, and, in the larger room at the end, an ottoman. I sat there while she nervously sorted through the clothes.

"They're fine," I said, more sharply than I'd ever spoken to her before. I took a breath. "Try this one on first."

I gave her a polo shirt. She hung it carefully on a hook, then looked at me. I nodded in encouragement. I wanted to see her undress. Pale, her fingers shaking, she began to undo the buttons of her blouse. She was deeply embarrassed, but I could see she was determined. I liked that very much. Underneath her blouse, she was wearing a camisole, and underneath that, a plain white bra. Something looked weird about it.

"Take that off and let me see it," I said. We hadn't talked about this, but now we were in it together. She was breathing more quickly and her skin flushing—not as red as I knew it could get, but pinker than usual.

"Yes, okay, I mean, of course, but I could keep it on and just try the shirt..."

"Shh," I said. "Sometimes people say, 'Yes, Ma'am.'"

"Yes, Ma'am," she whispered. She reached behind and unfastened the bra.

It was an ordinary underwire, or had been, but she'd altered it. The straps were folded over and firmly sewn down to shorten them, and the underwires had been removed, the holes neatly stitched up again.

"You sewed this?"

Heloise had her arms crossed in front of her chest. "Yes," she managed to say, her voice catching in her throat. "Mother taught me. All girls should know how to sew." She started to drop her arms, but then hugged herself miserably. "I'm sorry. What should I do now?"

"Just show me," I said. "I want to see."

She dropped her arms and stood up straighter. She revealed herself to me. I gazed at her small chest as I fingered the bra in my hands. Looking at it again, I saw that squares of felt had been sewn into the center of each cup.

"It's my best one," Heloise said quietly. "I always wear it when I go out. I don't like..." She looked down at her nipples, which were fully at attention in the cool, musty air of the dressing room.

"That's right," I said. "This is nicely done. You don't want people looking at your nipples."

Heloise gave me such a look of desperate relief that I felt my pussy clench. Really, I almost came. "I will look at your nipples, however," I said. "I am enjoying looking at your nipples right now."

For a moment, I thought Heloise would collapse right there on the floor, but she rallied. "How...?" she rasped.

I settled myself more comfortably on the ottoman. "Just

stand up straight and stay like that," I instructed. "Put your shoulders back more. Yes, that's right. That's very nice."

I looked at her nipples until she was trembling, and then I looked some more. I thought about how salty-sweet they would taste when I tongued them, how firm they would be when I put my lips around them, how they would throb and ache when I got her home and did to them whatever it was I had a mind to, involving perhaps hair clips or clothespins or twist ties.

"Breathe," I told her and she sobbed in a great gulp of air. I reached out a hand to her, and she grabbed it. Brought it to her lips.

"You're so beautiful," she said. "I'm sorry."

"For what?" Her mouth was soft on my palm.

"I'm too old. It's been too long."

"Nonsense. What matters is that you want to please me. Is that what you want, Heloise?"

"Cricket!" she burst out.

"What did you say?"

"Call me Cricket—it's my nickname. I hate being called Heloise!" She was trembling even more violently now, and starting to hunch over. I rested my hands on her hips and she calmed.

"Cricket. Do you want to please me? Answer the question."

"Yes, Ma'am! I do want to please you, of course I want to please you. I've only ever wanted to!"

"You do please me, Cricket. You have been a very good boi." I searched her face to see if she knew what I was talking about. I already knew she'd grown up and lived in a parallel world to mine, one where there was no queer theory, no talk of power dynamics, no *Best Lesbian Erotica* or being Facebook friends with Carol Queen. She just returned my gaze, undaunted, waiting for what I was going to say next.

"Take off your slacks."

Hastily, she slid the elastic waistband down her hips, unlaced her shoes and kicked them off. She got out of her slacks and threw them into a corner, eagerly straightening back up to face me in just her white anklets and a pair of the plain white underwear we had bought together.

"Your dainties, too," I said. "And do it nicely. This will be the last time you ever have to wear them." I had picked up a package of boxers for her.

Now her body was crimson. I was so pleased. I love a whole-body guy.

"Someone will come," she said, looking at the door.

"No one will come."

"But when I took Mother shopping here, someone always came to the door and asked, 'How are you doing?' They always did!"

"No one will come," I said again. "No one saw us. Now take them off."

"But I can't!"

"Why not?"

"I'm embarrassed."

"Why, Cricket?"

"I don't want you to see my, um, my…"

"Your?" I tapped my foot. I'm sure I was flushed, as well. It had been too long since I'd had a boi at my mercy like this.

"My, I forget what, I mean, my…"

"Just say it, Cricket."

"I can't!"

"Say it! What don't you want me to see?"

"I don't want you to see my front bottom, Ma'am!"

I couldn't help it, I let out a bark of laughter. "Your what?"

Redder and redder. "I'm sorry! I know there are other names for it, I, it's just, that's what Mother called it—please, can I leave my dainties on? I'll do whatever you want!"

"I want you to take them off."

The room was very quiet, just our labored breathing. I thought I might lose her. She looked over in the corner at her crumpled slacks and she looked at her bra, still on my knee. I didn't want to lose her.

"Cricket," I said softly. "Your dainties."

She took them off for me. Slowly. She did it as nicely as she could.

"Now touch it," I said when she was naked. "Touch it for me."

"It's private," she said.

"Not today. Today, I want to see you touch it."

"But Mother said it's private! To follow the rules of health, an occasional release is necessary, Ma'am, but in private! We, I mean, I could, would you let me..."

"Yes, Cricket, I will let you. But today, right here, I want to see you touch it. I want to see how you do it. It's not private today."

I was sure she had never done anything like this before. Who had been her lovers, during the sheltered, insular life she had told me about? I squeezed my legs together as she reached hesitantly down her belly, coming to rest with her fingers at the top of the sparse line of hair below her navel. I told her to go lower.

"Show me how you do it," I said again, then sighed with pleasure when she withdrew her hand and licked her fingers thoroughly before she began.

"Like this, Ma'am?" she asked, her voice rough. "You truly want to see me do this?"

"That's right. That's very good."

She resigned herself to it, steeled herself. It wasn't what she had been expecting. I don't know what she had been expecting, but she gave herself to me regardless. She started to jack off, knees slightly bent and apart, steadying herself against the wall with her other hand, her eyes never leaving mine. I could hear the small, wet, slapping sounds as she worked, see her gaze slacken as she got into it, hear her begin to make small, painful sounds in her throat. She moved closer to me, as if she couldn't help herself, and I let her stand between my knees. She was moving with more abandon now that she could read approval in my eyes. Her other hand slipped off the wall and I pinned her between my legs so she wouldn't fall. She struggled a little against me, squirming to get into the right position, the hand that had been on the wall gripping my shoulder. I could smell her excitement. I could almost taste it. I swallowed, licked my lips and brought my face to her chest. Her nipples were as succulent as I had imagined, and so sensitive. She shook and groaned at the feel of my tongue. I pulled her closer, kneading her ass, running my nails up and down the backs of her thighs. She was saying something, not words, just sounds. She let go of my shoulder, wet down all ten of her fingers and used both hands to bring herself off, leaning back, her crotch very close to my lips. Then her arms went around me in a desperate hug.

I pulled her into my lap and held her, my beautiful boi. She was shaking, tears running silently down her face. I wrapped her in my coat.

"Stay here."

I found the old queen dusting men's fragrances and paid for Heloise's new clothes. I gave her the boxers and a men's undershirt, had her put on the polo and a pair of khakis. I let her wear her old bra. When she was dressed, she carefully shook out my coat and helped me into it. She carried the bags, opened the doors for me and got me settled in the passenger seat of the Impala. It was very cold now, and fully dark. We drove through the city of Missoula, a valley where elk once wintered over and now 67,000 people live and dream and fight and fuck and go out for pizza. She looked so handsome in the light of the dash.

We didn't talk, although I could tell she was bursting to say something, anything, ask me what came next. But I knew she would wait. And when we got back to her quiet, orderly home in her quiet neighborhood, the one where she'd lived so long and so biddably with her mother, I would have no lack of instruction for her, my darling, my eager-to-please, my hungry, my newly-hatched boi.

NISRINE, INSIDE

Pavini Moray

Go ahead. Tell me to pick up that glass."

Nisrine's molten eyes fill with tears as her gaze drops to the half-finished plate of mosama bademjan on the table in front of her. We're eating at her favorite Persian restaurant, where the eggplant stew she is currently enjoying reminds her of her grandmother's. The way her long dark hair pours down her neck, slipping over her shoulders, I crave to push it back behind her delicate ear.

"There's a lot coming up for me. I don't think I can do this." Her tears slip out.

"It's very simple. Just look me in the eye, and push your will into me...make me want to do it for you."

Nisrine and I have been seeing each other regularly for about nine months. She is very like a child. She has toys that go everywhere with her, including a small stuffed tiger. She likes to make up science terms, and talk about astrology. She names all of her belongings. I'm not in love with her, but I adore her. She fucks with soft quick movements, and she's one of the few femmes

I've met who can make me, her Daddy, come. Being Daddy means taking good care of her precious desires, and holding her unfolding sexuality with tenderness.

"Pick up that glass!" she commands, like a feisty little dictator.

"Hmm, that was good, think you can slip in some sexy badass femme?" I purr.

"Pick up that glass, you filthy slut!" She's imitating every pro domme she's ever seen in a stupid movie that knows nothing about kink. I love watching her struggle.

"No, a little softer, more insinuating...make it so I can't resist."

"Would you pick up that glass?" Nisrine murmurs, her liquid eyes never leaving mine. Obligingly, I pick it up, and take a sip of water.

"Now, imagine telling my boi exactly how you'd like him to touch his clit."

Her gaze plummets immediately, and I take pity. Reaching across the table, I take her soft palm, turn it over and stroke the inside with my thumb. I look at her, without blinking, and watch as she does that thing I love; her eyes melting as she softens, and I can almost smell her pussy getting wet from where I sit across the table. My girl.

"You'll do just fine. I'll be right there, supporting you."

We'd been planning the seduction of my live-in boi Miki for hours, ever since she whispered into my ear that she'd like to try taking charge for once. I'd chuckled audibly when she asked if she could try to top me, but it got me thinking. This luscious, sexy woman who'd been trained growing up in the Middle East to be demur, feminine...there was no way she could authentically dominate me. But what a lovely desire. My mind turned to my good boi Miki. Maybe, just maybe I could help her to dominate him.

My boi Miki, with the solid broad shoulders of the swimmer that he'd once been, is in collared servitude to me. Miki would be easier for a novice to top, as he lives to submit. He's a ruthless badass housing rights trial lawyer by day, and collared submission gives him a place to set his great fight down, and surrender. Like Annie Lennox, circa 1988: tall, strong, feminine, masculine, in her uniform of tailored suit and tie.

Substitute sandy-brown hair and green eyes, that's Miki.

I keep him in strict chastity, and he is almost never allowed to let his fingers slip down between his legs, to finger his clit or to touch his pussy lips that are frequently slippery with want and need. He would be thrilled to submit to Nisrine if it was my will. Plus, he would be kind to her.

I drive Nisrine back to the home I share with Miki, who has not yet come home, and wait upstairs in the bedroom. It takes Nisrine forever in the bathroom to do whatever it is that femmes seem to need so much time to do. I identify as a Daddy. I'm pretty butch, but not adverse to a little glitter now and then. Okay, maybe a lot of glitter. But for tonight, I need nothing other than a quick shower. Plus, I already feel the wetness seeping from my cunt.

She knocks at the door lightly, and as she enters my eyes devour her—matching panties and bra, lace of course. Both the color of sweet cream, well made, and obviously new. Her alabaster skin contrasts sharply with her dark eyes and hair. Her nipples, now hidden by the bra but once rouged by me with her own lipstick, stand erect through the material. I trace the outline of the right nipple, and watch her shudder. I smirk at my ability to make goose bumps rise over her body with such a light caress. She smells of roses and frangipani. I pull her to me.

I lay her down on the bed and pet her into relaxation, kissing and teasing at the edge of the fabric of her bra. I gradually work my fingers under the bra, until I grasp and fondle her hidden nipple. She starts in on her sweet sighs, but I have to pull back before she's fully gone into sexy land. We have work to do.

We go over the plan again. When my boi arrives home, she will go to greet him, and inform him that he is to come to the bedroom. I will place his collar around his neck, snap his leash into place. And then, to his complete surprise, he will be invited to sit in a chair at the foot of the bed, while Nisrine holds his leash.

And then, if it pleases her, he will be granted permission to touch himself while she and I have sexy time and he watches. His masturbation will be at her discretion, at her desire. Inside, I am nervously excited about his surprise, of my allowing him to be used in this way. It's not happened before.

This is nervousness that I will never show. Her own nervousness is apparent. We talk about it, this desire of hers to dominate, to be in control. Tears come, again, as she talks about her family, her role and the role of women in the Persian culture. She doesn't agree with everything in the upbringing she's had, but still, it's hard to undo three decades of training.

At last, her words fall away, and she lies there in my bed, gazing up at me with those eyes that contain the world, at least for tonight. Her breath is coming quickly, and it quickens in her chest even more when we hear my boi returning home. We give him a few minutes to arrive, and then she looks at me, asking me with her eyes if the time is now. I nod, and she gets up.

"Don't engage him in any conversation. No questions. Quietly command his presence in the bedroom." She looks scared but so sexy and the combination is so hot I feel the searing flame in my junk turn up a notch. I watch her full ass as she pads softly away from me and down the hall, and think nasty thoughts about that ass until she returns, with Miki in tow, his tie loosened.

He looks amused, and curious. So far, so good. I tell him to undress. He and I have been texting during the day, so he knows there is some surprise in store. He's asked me to please make him jealous. In the way we've worked out our relationship, he is monogamous to me, while I can be intimate with others.

Perhaps unfair, this arrangement serves us well in the way it reinforces our power dynamic. And even though we have agreed for it to be like this after long discussion, jealousy still comes up for him, especially about Nisrine.

He's met her several times before, though only in social contexts. What he's noticed is that feeling jealous actually intensifies his sexual arousal. He loves to think about me fucking other people, and gets turned on by it, while simultaneously being powerless to jerk off or get any relief. He has struggled with my relationship with Nisrine, even as he's fantasized about it. I know he's contemplated getting to watch me fuck her many times, and his face betrays his turn-on.

I watch, as Miki slowly peels off the layers of lawyer armor. The expensive silk tie. The starched white shirt, still crisp even after the day. The belt buckle. The suit pants. The black socks, with sock garters. Finally, he's standing there in his own French black lingerie that I insist he wear under his suit. We have a ritual. He is to undress only to this point, and I do the rest.

He turns around so that I can unfasten his bra. I take my time and slip my hands under the silk, cupping his small breasts. His nipples harden under my touch. Removing his bra, I place the heavy black leather collar around his neck, lingering with the buckle. As I snap the leash into place, I get the twinge in my pussy that I always get when I put it on him.

"This boi is mine," I murmur.

He stands straight as I ease his panties over his slim hips and brush my fingers over his neatly trimmed bush. I smell his excited smell. He would never in a million years suggest the situation that he now finds himself in. Left to his own accord, he would be drinking a single malt scotch, studying.

Nisrine very politely asks him if he'd prefer to sit at the side of the bed, or at the foot, and suggests that he move the wooden straight-back chair to the foot when he indicates his preference.

"I want you to have a good view," she says insinuatingly.

I see him inhale sharply. He's already picked up on the sex smell in the room, and the candles all around definitely indicate that something pleasurable has been going on.

I watch as the cool leather around his neck softens him, cracks away the veneer he has to wear as a lawyer in the world. The collar strips him bare of all of that, and leaves his essential, people-pleasing self naked and vulnerable for us to see.

"We are going to have sex. And you are going to watch. And if I like how you are watching, I will let you touch yourself. Do you understand? Don't be too creepy." Nisrine seems in control, and while her tone might be slightly sharper than one I would use with Miki (he's very well-trained, after all) it's still pretty good for a first attempt. Leash in hand, she glares at him strictly, and then rolls over into my arms.

"How am I doing?" she whispers into my ear, too soft for him to hear.

I smile into her neck, and nuzzle and lick at her earlobe, so that she begins to coo. I can hear Miki's breath already. He has a tendency to breathe hard and fast, as soon as he is the slightest bit aroused. The transition of Miki from powerful broker of justice into the aroused, panting submissive boi never fails to make the hunger for him rise up strongly in me. I allow Miki's turned-on breathing to fuel my own turn-on.

I palm Nisrine's large breasts, still encased in creamy lace, and trace the edges across the top, fingertips playing with her nipples, until the tissue responds and becomes erect. She's moaning like crazy, and every once in a while giving a jerk on

Miki's leash. I bury my face between her breasts, and my mind flashes to wondering how it is for Miki, to see me take such pleasure in another woman.

Nisrine's pussy smells different from any pussy I've ever smelled. Perhaps it's the spices she uses in her cooking. She prepares her own advieh, a Persian spice mixture made of black pepper, cinnamon, cardamom, star anise and nutmeg among other things. Perhaps it is her unique biology. Whatever the reasons, her ripe, pungent smell almost vibrates the air. While Miki and I are both frequently wet, I wasn't exaggerating when I said I could almost smell her getting turned on from across the table.

I trail my hands down her lush body, tracing the edges of her dainty panties before running my index finger gently across her mons and dipping down to the moist valley between her lips. I can play with her pussy like this for hours, her moaning, me thrusting my hips gently as I tease her covered labia. But tonight, her panties aren't just moist, they are sopping wet. My fingers slip and slide over the silky material, and I can feel the pull of her cunt wanting to be fucked.

I've been ignoring Miki, but she hasn't.

"Open your eyes, I want you to look!" Nisrine is tracking everything he does. He is cooperating.

"You can touch yourself now, but don't you *dare* come before I do!" she intones severely.

He looks to me for confirmation, and at my subtle nod, his fingers dive into his vulva, grab at the clitoris he likes to call his cock and start stroking vigorously, panting and moaning all the while. I can only imagine how jealous he is feeling, watching Nisrine receive all of my touch and attention while I pay him none.

Nisrine is ready to be fucked. We've been talking, plotting, playing, kissing and teasing for hours. The moment is here. She takes off her panties, and Miki's moans kick into high gear as he catches sight of her soaking, engorged pussy.

"Tell him to shut up," I suggest, reveling in the reaction Miki is having. I lean toward her and whisper in her ear, "And then stuff your panties in his mouth so he can't talk." She delicately rolls the bit of soaking lace and shoves it into his open mouth. His surprise is palpable, and the heat between my own thighs increases. He begins to slurp and suck at the panty gag. He is so into it, I almost start to laugh.

Turning my attention back to Nisrine's cunt, I begin to slide my index finger up and down the sides of her bare labia, relishing the exquisite softness of her skin. Her hips make little beckoning movements. Although she wants desperately for me to fuck her, it's easier for her to tell Miki to shut up than it is to ask me to put my fingers inside of her. I relent, and slide my index and middle fingers into her, meanwhile massaging her clit with my thumb.

Miki is going nuts attacking his pussy and yanking at his little cock fiercely. I don't know that I've ever seen him so turned on. His eyes are glued to her pussy, my fingers and her gushing fluid. Pulling my fingers out quickly, I feed him a bit of her juices, letting him lick my fingers clean. He looks sufficiently grateful to be allowed to participate.

I love the playful, childlike part of Nisrine. Tonight, she's brought with her a short, fat rainbow dildo that she wants me to stuff into her pussy. She calls it "Moana." She is both innocent and worldly at the same time. Both turn me on.

Teasing her lips with its width for a moment, I allow the brightly colored fat dildo to slowly enter her and be swallowed by the depths of her cunt. I don't need to look at Miki to know he is practically frothing at the mouth. I smile, fantasizing about his lawyer buddies seeing him now.

Her hips move to meet the fluid movements of my hand

holding her cock, as Miki grabs and rubs his own miniature cock. His chair is rocking and hitting the wall in time with the rhythm of our fuck. Nisrine opens her legs even farther, giving him full view of her drenched pussy, surrounded by a dense forest of dark, damp curls. Suddenly, she stops moving as her back arches and she throws her head back. I feel the clench of her pussy muscles as she comes and I hold my breath, feeling my own pussy throb in tandem. Her orgasm is long and powerful. Time stands still.

When it's over, she puts her hand over mine, and removes the cock from her steaming hole.

"I want him to suck it."

Her voice is quietly firm, and I sense the seriousness of her desire. "Make him take it." The rainbow toy is glistening with her nectar. Nodding, I move it slowly toward his mouth. With my other hand, I remove Nisrine's panties, absolutely soaking with Miki's saliva. They are hot and damp in my hand, and I feel sad to throw them on the floor. I place them on the bed instead.

Miki's aquamarine eyes never leave the cock slowly approaching his swollen mouth. He tilts his pretty head back, and his mouth opens to accept my girl's cock, dripping and warm from her cunt. We don't play much with dildo cocks, and he struggles to take it all the way in. His face contorts, and wet gagging sounds issue from his throat. His eyes are slightly bulging, and yet his face leans into the cock, urgently trying to take in all of the thickness that was recently buried in Nisrine's pussy.

"If I can take it, so can you," Nisrine taunts, and something deep in my loins stirs at hearing my sweet, demur girl talk dirty to my nasty, well-trained submissive boi. I ease the cock down Miki's throat, and watch as his eyes seek hers. Tears fill his eyes as he sucks and laps her cock, and his own hands fall still in his lap as he honors her dominance. She's made him cry.

I see that faraway look in his damp eyes, the one he gets in our best scenes, and I sense his complete calm and surrender. Glancing at Nisrine, I notice her fingers tracing her labia, gently teasing her hole and her clit. She pulls his leash taut.

"Stroke yourself, and let me see you come."

As she says this, a flash of fear passes over Miki's face. He knows he is to come only for me. I watch as his mind begins to react, pulling him out of the delirious subspace I love to see him in. Thinking quickly, I consider what I want. Nisrine is unaware that he is not allowed to come for anyone but me. She wants him to come. I want her to succeed in this first attempt at domination. And when I breathe into my own hot desire, I want to watch my boi come with his own fingers, something he is almost never allowed to do. I feel his eyes on me.

"It's okay; I want to watch you come. And when you come, I want you to send your orgasm straight down your leash, and into Nisrine's hands." Miki visibly relaxes, as I continue to ease the cock in and out of his soft mouth. I remove it, and sniff to make sure he has cleaned off all of Nisrine's juices.

Miki's hands ease back down between his muscular legs, and he begins to stroke himself slowly, easing three fingers of one hand into his hungry cunt, and slowly fucking himself. I know he's rubbing his own G-spot, his favorite. His eyes start to close but snap open as he remembers Nisrine's desire for him to keep them open. He drops them to her pussy and licks his lips.

I imagine he's fantasizing about touching her, touching her where my fingers are softly playing. His touch remains slow and constant, and the frantic bucking of earlier has passed. His breathing quickens, but he is quiet as he brings himself to the brink of orgasm. I feel it in my own cunt, his pleasure, and when he starts to come, he gazes into Nisrine's lovely face.

He allows her to see him coming, eyes open, because I have wanted it. He is raw, vulnerable and open. His cum flows freely from his cunt, dripping down between the cheeks of his taut ass as his large clitoris quivers in the candlelight. The orgasm energy he sends down the leash into her waiting hands is almost visible, and her hands tremble to receive it. Quiet descends on the room. The smell of sex is thick. Wet cunts, flushed faces, swollen lips of pussies and mouths.

In a moment, they will both turn to me, wanting to demonstrate their gratitude that I am their Daddy, that I take care of their desires, and provide for their pleasure. I will allow them to service me with their sticky fingers, their ripe mouths. I will accept the caresses of my boi, and of my girl, and I will accept the offerings of their bodies, surrendering to mine. After I've been pleasured, I know we will sleep, all together, Nisrine in my arms, Miki at my feet. I could get used to sharing a bed with my boi and girl.

GARGOYLE LOVERS

Sacchi Green

'm siingin' in the raaiin..." But that song was from the wrong Gene Kelly movie, and it wasn't quite raining, and I was only whistling. My speaking voice gets me by, but singing blows the whole presentation.

Hal glanced down, her face stern in that exaggerated way that makes me tingle in just the right places. I shoved my hands into my pockets, skipped a step or two, and knew she felt as good as I did. Hal's hardly the type to dance through the Paris streets like Gene Kelly, especially across square cobblestones, but there was a certain lilt to her gait.

Or maybe a swagger. "That pretty-boy waiter was all over you," I said slyly. A gay guy making a pass always makes her day. "And giving me dirty looks every chance he got!"

"Lucky for you I'm not cruising for pretty boys, then. But don't give me too much lip or I might change my mind."

I couldn't quite manage penitence, but at least I knew better than to remind her that she already had a pretty boy, for better or worse. Still, some punishment games would be a fine end to the evening. Last night we'd been too jet-lagged to take proper advantage of the Parisian atmosphere. "That maître d' with a beak like a gargoyle was sure eyeing me, too, especially from behind." I gave another little skip.

Hal ignored the bait. "Thought you'd had your fill of gargoyles today." A cathedral wouldn't have been her first choice for honeymoon sightseeing, but the mini-balcony of our rental apartment had a stupendous view of Notre-Dame de Paris. I'd oohed and ahhed about gargoyles over our croissants and café au lait, so she'd humored me and we'd taken the tour.

To tell the truth, being humored by Hal unnerved me a bit. I didn't want being married to make a difference in our relationship. The fact that she'd shooed me out of that sex toy shop in Montmartre while she made a purchase was reassuring, but just in case, I decided I could manage some genuine penitence after all.

I hung my head and peered up at her slantwise. "I know I was a real pain. I can't figure out what it is about gargoyles that just gets to me. They're sort of scary, but not really, and sort of sad, and some of them are beautiful in a weird kind of way." Just as Hal was, but I'd never say so. "I'm sorry I went on about them like that."

"What makes you think they're sad? Just because their butts are trapped in stone?" She was trying to suppress a grin. I felt better.

"Well, I'd sure hate that, myself!"

That got me the squeeze on my ass I'd been angling for. "I'd rather have these sweet cheeks accessible," she said. The squeeze got harder than I'd bargained for, startling me into a grimace.

She eased off with a slow stroke between my thighs. "You should've seen your face just now. Could be there's something like that going on with the gargoyles. Not rage, or fear, or pain at all—unless it's pain so delicious it makes them howl with lust."

I was awestruck. Hal is generally the blunt, taciturn type, but I love it when her wicked imagination bursts forth. Almost as much as I love the vulnerability that once in a while gives an extra gruffness to her voice.

She was on a roll now, face alight like a gleeful demon's. A lovable demon. "There's somebody hidden behind the stone, in another dimension, or time, or whatever, giving the gargoyle the fucking of its life. A reaming so fine it's been going on for centuries."

"Yes!" I was very nearly speechless. To lean out high above Paris, in the sun, wind and rain of eons, my face forever twisted in a paroxysm of fierce joy while Hal's thrusts filled me eternally with surging pleasure...

A few drops of rain began to fall, but that wasn't what made us hurry across the Pont de Saint-Louis. The great ornate iron gates at our apartment building had given me fantasies that morning of being chained, spread-eagled, against them, but now I rushed across the cobblestoned courtyard and through the carved oak door, so turned on that the four flights of stairs inside scarcely slowed me down—which might also have been because Hal's big hand on my butt was hurrying me along.

At our apartment, though, she held me back while she opened the door. "Over-the-threshold time. It'll be more official when we get back home, but this will have to do for now."

So I entered the room slung over Hal's shoulder, kicking a little for balance, until she dumped me amongst the red and gold brocade cushions on the couch. They went tumbling off as I struggled to get my pants lowered.

"Not here," she mused. "Maybe up there?" There was a sturdy railing across the loft that held the king-sized bed.

"Out there! Please?" The balcony was really only a space where the French windows were set back into the wall about a foot, but there was an intricate iron fence along the edge, and with the windows wide open it had felt like balcony enough at breakfast time.

"Can you be quiet as a gargoyle?"

"You can gag me."

"No. I want to see your face." Hal pulled open the windows, grabbed the bag from the sex toy store, heaved me up, and the next minute I was kneeling on the balcony and clutching the fence.

She moved aside a couple of pots of geraniums and tested the fence for strength and anchoring. "This would take even my weight," she muttered. In seconds she'd fastened my wrists to the railing with brand new bonds that looked uncannily like chains of heavy iron links, even though they weren't hard as metal and had just a hint of stretch to them. "Feel enough like a gargoyle?"

"Mm-hm." I was drifting into a space I'd never known before. Lights from the Quai D'Anjou below and the *quais* across the Seine were reflected on the dark river, flickering like ancient torches as the water rippled past. Even the lights of modern Paris on the far bank took on a mellow glow that could have fit into any century.

"Hold that thought." Hal backed away into the room. I scarcely heard the rustling of the shop bag or the running of water in the bathroom. Then she was back, soundlessly, a dark looming presence that might have been made of stone.

The night air drew me into its realm. I leaned out over the railing as far as my bonds would allow, my butt raised high. Then Hal had one arm around my waist, holding me steady, while her other hand probed into my inner spaces that she knew so well. Need swelled inside me and shuddered through my body, catching in my throat as strangled, guttural groans. My face twisted with the struggle not to make too much noise, my mouth gaped open and my head flailed back and forth.

A whimper escaped when her hand withdrew, and so did a short, sharp bleat as something new replaced it; smooth, lubed, not quite familiar, not any of Hal's gear I'd felt before. I heard her heavy breathing, felt her thrusts and lost all sense of anything beyond the moment, anything beyond our bodies. A scream started forcing its way up through my chest and throat.

Just in time, Hal snapped open the bonds on my wrists, lifted me from behind and lurched with me across the plump back of the couch. With a rhythm accelerating like a Parisienne's motorbike she finished me off, then found her own slower, deep pace, and her own release. I could still barely breathe, but I managed to twist my neck enough to see her contorted face at that moment. Yes, magnificently beautiful in its own feral way.

In the aftermath we curled together, laughing when she showed me the new gargoyle-faced dildo slick with my juices. "Those French don't miss a trick when it comes to tourists," I said.

Hal grew quiet. I thought she was dozing, but after a while she cleared her throat. "Those French..." Her voice was unusually gruff. She tried again. "They claim to be tops in the lover department, too, I've heard. But I've got the best deal in the whole world with you. The best lover..." She stroked my still-simmering pussy. "The prettiest boy..." She touched my cheek. "The best wife... And the wildest gargoyle in all of France."

I remembered her face just minutes ago, and knew that the last part wasn't true. Still, the wisest response seemed to be a kiss that moved eventually from her mouth along her throat, and lower, and lower, with more daring than I'd ever risked before; eventual proof that the best lover part, at least, was absolutely certain.

HER
GARDENER'S
BOY

D. Orchid

I bit my lip, nodding my head to the beat of my own quick pulse as I forced myself to sit reasonably still and watch the western garden wall for signs of my usual summer visitor. The early afternoon sun warmed my skin, the smooth wooden slats of the park-like bench pressed neat dents into my rear end, and I wondered if she'd be different this time. Would she ring the bell out front instead, like a university type should? Like what my mum called a "proper lady?" Would she even come at all?

I was clean enough, I thought, had run fingers through my cropped-short hair, and left the glass door open with only the screen pulled shut, separating our garden from the house, just in case she came by way of the front door. She never had, of course, but she could and I didn't want to miss her. It might be her first time inside the actual house since she'd come calling years ago when freedom from parental eyes was still new to us both. Looking down at me from the wall she'd scaled from outside, she'd asked, rather more confidently than I could manage, "Who are you? And what on earth are you doing to those flowers?"

Though I could never quite retrieve the thoughts I had in those early moments, somehow I let her stay and she decided to come back every summer afternoon that she could get away. I listened and I learned and I'd never worried in the interim that she might not return.

Now, however, with a year of uni in her pocket, I wasn't sure what to expect. My thighs were tight with tension, ready to spring toward the door or just pace about the garden, siphoning off the energy that trickled out in my mindless rocking and the near-obsessive way I strained at every sound. Was that a knock? Footsteps? That brushing? What could that be?

When I finally saw tan fingers gripping the top of the wall beside tossed-up thin-strapped sandals, I knew everything I needed to let me breathe, to free my lip from the rein of my teeth and curve my mouth into a smile of relief. Her arm and leg, head and torso, came into view, hugging the wall, and the sunlight striking my face turned my shadowed doubts into harmless flecks of dust floating in the air between us. She sat up on the wall as if it were the queen's throne itself and grinned at me like I was the whole of England.

I swore for a moment that someone had buttered my heart and put it in the oven to bake like cookies. Had it gotten this hot in the span of three blinks? Maybe it had.

When she worked her way down the inside of the wall, however, deftly avoiding anything that might snag her flowing skirt, I didn't have to be told to rise. As she strode my way, sandals swinging in the crook of her fingers, I was already on my feet, beaming back at her like it had been more than just nine months between our last visit and now.

Even curvier and stronger of arm than I remembered, Aniah was tall and radiantly olive-toned with dark hair that still shined enough to draw my gaze when her own arresting deep-brown eyes let mine go. Her gravitational pull even had me leaning forward, like the planets in my da's telescope. So I asked myself, for what felt like the hundredth time, why I bothered with my mum's social experiments during the year.

Putting on nice pants, suffering a curling iron in my hair and letting a boy from across the river take me out did not a "proper girl" make me. Nor did it make me want to "soften up," as mum suggested, entirely too regularly, as if smothering me with pink lace would snuff out the rougher bits and only leave "an eligible young miss" for her to court out to every son-of-a-friend who'd take me off her hands. The fact that I was stuck in the house even after my final exam year just made me more adamant about it all, though, not less. It was why I'd waited this afternoon, why I'd hoped and why I'd work on my knees in the dirt for this eccentric girl—woman, now—who climbed over my garden wall each summer.

Her eyes slid over my sun-battered face, my T-shirt with a fraying collar, my rolled-up-cuff overalls and my already-dirty kicks, and her smile never wavered. All she said was: "You look ready to work, boy. Am I correct?"

"Yes, miss." I squared my shoulders and lifted my chin, ready and waiting for orders. It didn't matter that I didn't want to be a real boy. When she was here, this was her garden and I was just her gardener's boy.

"Well then," Aniah said with a gorgeous smirk draped across her lips and a sparkle of fun in her eyes, "about these rose bushes..."

Her voice and the implicit arrangement she hadn't forgotten or tossed aside sent the swirl of worry and want in my stomach surging up to smack me in the chest, my breath pressing out all at once. "Yes, miss." I nodded, trying to remember to draw new air in and let it out again, tipping my head toward the row of pink flowering bushes near the bench. "Those there?"

"Yes." She pursed her lips as she assessed the bushes and

then me again, a curious quirk in her eyebrow that I couldn't quite decipher. "It's a good place to start. I want to see your work up close today."

"Is that so?" I didn't have a hat to tip, but I nodded again, something more like a bow, and stepped aside to allow her to walk up to the bench before I bent to retrieve the gloves and tools I'd brought out from the shed. "A trim then, miss?"

"Yes," she said, as perfect as a painter's model, upright and yet somehow relaxed on the bench with her head tilted to regard the bushes in question. "Make them shapely, like bowls, a bit more rounded."

I went to them and down on my knees beside them, but found myself waiting again for some reason.

"Go ahead. I trust you." She nudged me gently with her toes, her voice soft and encouraging in ways that made warmth swim across my shoulders, knowing her eyes were taking in the curve of my back.

I twisted around to lift my eyes to hers, unsure how to tell her I was grateful that, even after her first year really quite far away, she'd come back to...be with me this way. It didn't quite feel like play anymore, like when we were children and youths, but I wanted it, needed it, all the same.

Her smile turned knowing, her eyes like crystalized syrup, flashing nature's sweetness at me. "Is there a problem, boy?"

"No, miss." I shook my head. "I'll do it however you like. Whatever you like." Not just these bushes, I meant, though I couldn't explain that all out loud. This garden, or me, or the world. In that moment, I might have meant them all.

"Yes." She nodded, a more serious and thoughtful expression on her face than I'd seen before, her voice still soft but firmer somehow, as if she'd considered this all a long time ago. "However I like and whatever I like."

My heart skidded with her eyes on me like that and even

fully clothed, I felt like my skin was bare to her eyes. The stirring summer wind wasn't enough to cool the fire she left burning there.

"Now get to it, boy. We'll talk later."

Work first, I knew that, and I lowered my eyes respectfully. "Yes, miss."

Starting my work and continuing it about the garden as directed was as thrilling as always, maybe more so, and I felt sure my pulse was going to dance its way out of my skin when she rose from her customary seat to start walking about the garden as I moved from place to place. She strolled past me here and there, her skirts brushing my clothing in ways that made me worry on occasion that they would get dirty, though I said nothing of my thoughts to her. It was her garden right then and she could do as she liked.

When she began to run her fingers through my short but layered hair while I worked, however, I froze at first, unsure of myself, unsure of her. She had only ever touched me, even just playfully, when we were both ensconced on the bench, just two youths murmuring to each other about funny stories and oddball parents. Her touches were always fond, but this was... out of routine. I didn't know what that meant.

"Boy, am I distracting you?"

I took a breath, but shook my head, resuming the work of setting a growing plant into its new home in the sparsest patch of the garden. "No, miss."

It wasn't just my hair, however, and as the moments went by and I moved from task to task, she touched my cloth-covered shoulders, slid fingers down my arm, brushed her thumb against my nape and even traced the curve of my ear until I shuddered and really did have trouble concentrating. It made me realize what was different about these touches. They were no less fond than they'd been in the summer before, but she touched me now as she did the real inhabitants of the garden, the lilacs and roses, the hydrangeas, the leafy ferns.

She touched me like I was a prized part of her garden and like she had every right to run her fingers over anywhere on me she found smooth or rough or just interesting. Because I was here, as true as the small trees that had been growing since our earliest days together, and because when she walked the stone paths here, she was mistress of this garden. Every inch belonged to her and that also seemed to mean every inch of me.

When she finally had me stop for the day, my heartbeat fluttered in my chest and along every expanse of skin that she had touched. Every inch under my clothes where her fingers left a trail sparked with heat. I could even feel traces of her in all the places that I'd hoped or feared she would touch, even if she never did. Standing to face her as instructed was surreal, the flush deep in my cheeks, and I couldn't have raised my eyes to meet hers even if I'd wanted to. I wasn't wholly embarrassed exactly, but I was something, something hot and wondrous, something I both wanted more of and wasn't sure I could handle.

"Boy, do you like pleasing me?"

"Very much, miss." I couldn't and wouldn't deny that.

"And if I were to teach you other ways to please me, would you learn?"

I wasn't entirely sure what she could mean, but I nodded slowly, giving the question due thought. "I would try my best, miss."

She touched my face then, for the first time that day, for the first time in nine months, and I closed my eyes at how it felt to be so gently caressed by someone who saw me and didn't shame me for it. Whatever else she might be, she was someone who cared for me in her own strange way and thought my strangeness and skills were worthwhile, were interesting. They were even enough to make her bide her time and clear what easily could have been suitor-full schedules to dally in the back garden with me—for no reason I could surmise past her love of nature's beauty and something she liked about my company.

Softly, her body so close to me that I was sure the sun shone from her skin for all the heat she drew along mine, she leaned in and said, "Do you dream of me when I'm away?"

My chest was a fist clenching tight around nothing but air, empty enough to ache as I closed my eyes and willed myself not to fear that she would run if I were honest. "Every day." The words came out rough, leaving my throat the same.

"Then we'll make this a dream to remember."

When she kissed me, her lips were soft and warm and sure, even if my own were chapped and unstudied. It meant I didn't have to look at her with wet eyes, though, or answer with the words that were trapped in my stomach. *I love you,* I thought as I let her kiss me and I kissed her back, cautious and uncertain, working not to let the full swell of my desire press against her, overwhelming her like the men on the street whose rowdy flirtations had always made me want to sink into my shoes. She deserved better. I just wasn't sure how to offer it to her.

I parted my lips for her and let her show me what it was to kiss with tongues shared between mouths, teeth dragged over lips and a gentle suck that left my lips thick and tingly hot when she finally pulled away. I was glad to be able to look at her with dry eyes then, my shoulders relaxed, less tense with worry, and the smile she shared, only a few centimeters down from my own, made me feel like I had swallowed flower bulbs at breakfast. With her sun and water and care, there was a garden blooming in me, just for her.

"There's more if you're willing."

"For you, I'm always willing."

She actually blushed and I couldn't help the spread of a roguish grin across my lips. She just raised an eyebrow, laughter on her tongue, and grabbed my hand, dragging me back to our bench. There she pushed me down to sit and stood before me. "Ladies first, of course."

There'd be no debate about that from me. I might have been a female, but I was surely not a lady. "Of course...miss?"

I made the title a question as I wasn't sure if we had graduated to something else or if this new style of interaction was in our usual mode. I rather liked our usual mode, but the novelty and heat of this new adventure was enough to ease my way past our routine. She just smirked, though, and lifted her chin in the manner of an olden-day aristocrat.

"Yes, boy. Now help me with this skirt."

I drew in breath and let it out, nodding for two beats too many as I reacquired my shocked-away mind, my words shaky. "As you like, miss."

She took both of my hands in hers and set them at the base of her skirt, just below her knees, dragging them both up the outside of her thighs until her skirts bunched at her waist, her own hands balling up the fabric at each hip as I let my hands fall away. I didn't mean to stare at her simple pale-green underwear, but the sight of them and the bare curves of her body made the wire connecting my brain and my bits flame to life like the filament of a lightbulb.

I glanced up at her and then back down at the soft-looking green set against soft-looking skin and wondered what it would be like to lean in and nuzzle her there, to feel the soft of each against my cheeks. Whatever she saw when I looked up again made her nod, her small smile with parted lips a gilded invitation.

"Go on then. Get close."

Even brushing my lips against her thighs, extra warm from the brisk way she'd walked us back to the bench, I still couldn't have imagined the scent of her, a mix of sharp like vinegar and musky-sweet like smoke and maple sap. It made my mouth water, but it was my nose brushing against that heat, breathing her in, that sent a shudder through me. Rubbing my lips over the cotton, my face tucked tight between her legs, I wasn't sure I even had to open my mouth to drown in her. I wanted to, though, and when she bunched the held-up parts of her skirt in one hand and ran free fingers through my hair, I waited for her cue, just mouthing her and listening to the soft pump of her breath and the sway of many well-tended leaves.

"Use your mouth."

Even still sure and strong, her voice had grown into something full of heavy breaths and barely held-back moans. I could hear the thump-thump-thump of my own heartbeat along the side of my neck and in a winding line up to my temple, but her breath was the rhythm to which I set my exploration. Open-mouthed, I started at the top of the crease I had molded into her folds with just the pressure of my eager lips, the tip of my tongue pausing as I found a supple rigid nub, massaging it until her hips began to shift, left and then right and then she was pressing me in, her hand at the back of my head as she groaned over me.

When her fingers tightened in my hair, though, clenching but not yet tugging, I wasn't sure if I should keep going or stop and my ministrations stuttered. "Did I tell you to stop?" She shook my head slightly in reprimand, the ache and total rule in it making my own moan slip over my lips.

I didn't have to hear any more, however, as she said, so breathy it was a wonder she could still stand up, "Be a good boy for me."

I made my "Yes, miss," a trick with my tongue, a flick that had her crying out and dumping her skirt over my head as she gripped my shoulder with her newly empty hand. Even her curses were beautiful and as I sucked and licked her there, tasting as much wet cloth as her, I resented the barrier, but I was grateful even for this chance to please her so intimately, to make more of my body useful and worth something to her.

I knew what was coming as her sounds, mixed with encouragements and sharp staccato swears, became a string of "Yes yes yes yes." I couldn't get enough of it in my ears, wanted to hear that litany every morning, evening and every afternoon, and in my dreams I wanted to be deeper even than I was right then, somehow so profoundly in the middle of it, wrapped up and surrounded by it. My body cried "Yes" as hers did, desperate to taste the culmination of her use of me, desperate to watch her race up the mountain, jump off it and fly. And when she finally came it was with a shout that scared nearby birds into a flutter of worried wings.

Crushed close there for more breaths than I had air for, I felt so thoroughly kept, trapped and held by her thighs, her hands, her skirt and her ever-wetter heat, and though I whimpered at the force of her body's reaction, I wasn't sure I ever wanted her to let me go. Dizzy and so hot between my own legs by the time she started to relax around me again, I was painfully grateful for the bench under me. When she spoke, though, exhaling slowly and gently combing down my hair with her fingers, pulling us apart, I knew I would have to do more and I wasn't at all sure how I would manage. By her will, apparently, and my will to please her.

"I want more from you, boy. Will you give me more?"

"Yes, miss," I panted, hauling in air as quietly as I could to replenish my supply.

Her skirt was back in place now, flowing subtly with the breeze in front of me, but I knew exactly what it hid, the seafoam green of her knickers dark underneath, edging toward a stormier color, like leaves shifting from the new buds of spring to the hunter of late summer. Looking up into her eyes, at the smile on her face, I felt dizzy all over again and tried not to imagine how such an immense and vibrant presence would fit in my room, or even really in my house. The open spaces of the garden suited her so much better than any place I could construct in my dazed mind.

"If you kneel on the walkway, I'll take the bench and show you what I mean."

"Of course, miss." It was a simple answer, yes, but my heart and breath were running toward some finish line I couldn't see. I stood and stepped aside for the second time that afternoon, but both that and finding my knees felt different now, a cool breeze down my back reminding me that we were doing these things out in the open. I didn't want to stop, though. This was where she should be pleased, pleasured, worshipped. I just couldn't wrap my mind around what more I could offer her, what more I could do.

She sat with legs spread but coyly, her skirt falling over her knees and showing me no more than she wanted me to see right then. "Had you been playing in the garden before you began your work for me today?"

"No, miss." My eyebrows dipped inward as I looked up at her, wondering where this was going or what that meant to her.

"Good. Then come here and help me out of these undies." She smirked. "You got them all wet."

One corner of my mouth quirked up and I politely refrained from mentioning that she hade done a fair amount of the work herself. This time I only nudged her skirt up enough to get my hands comfortably beneath it, following the tops of her thighs until I could grip the waistband of the offending material and tug. Hooking my fingers in and dragging the cloth down, I watched and felt her lift her hips, my bottom lip snagging on my teeth again as I thought about what it might look like to watch her touch herself, the smoothness of her tan calves only making the image more vivid.

"Want to feel what a mess you made?" With the damp fabric bunched beside her on the bench, she took my hand and guided it under her skirt and up to touch the heat still gathered there, the backs of my knuckles sliding through slick warmth that seemed well worth exploring.

"We're going to get your skirt wet instead." I hadn't realized how husky my voice had gone until the words were already slipping past the opening of my mouth, but I saw and felt the way she pressed up against my fingers in answer.

"I don't mind." Her breath steeped her words with want and I wondered if she'd let me under her skirt again to swallow more of her lush heat. "Do you ever put your fingers inside?"

For a moment, I hesitated, unsure which answer to give. "Not usually, no." Was that strange? I wasn't sure, but I just… preferred outside stimulation more than anything else. Her smile and one-shoulder shrug put me at ease, though.

"But if I let you put your fingers in me, that would be okay?" The way her smile had shifted to a coy smirk told me she knew the answer already, but wanted me to say it anyway.

I fluttered my fingers against her folds, making her breath catch as we held each other's eyes. "Very much so…if you'll direct me."

"Always."

The word sunk into my chest and stayed, not like a sword but like a jewel too heavy and too precious to lift. Licking my lips, I waited for her word.

"Just one to start." She rocked gently against my fingers. "But make sure it's wet."

I wasn't sure how it could be anything but with the subtle flow of her juices tripping over my skin, but I slid my first two fingers down between her folds and then up again. Teasing her nub before slipping through that silken track to zero in on the source of her heat, one finger circling and then slowly pressing into her. I found my other hand on her knee as her legs fell wider apart, her hips angling her body up to take my seeking finger, thrusting up around it in shallow shifts of up and down.

"Did I give you permission to put your hand there?" She panted the question, but still managed to make me feel terribly forward, the heat in my cheeks from a mixture of things this woman lit up inside me.

"No, miss." I began to pull my hand away, fingertips lingering despite my desire to be good.

"Put it behind your back." I slid it behind with a square bend at the elbow like I'd seen soldiers do on the telly. "Yes, like that. And give me another."

The subtle pull in my shoulder only made me feel more hers, more fully physically under her control, and I slid a second finger in with my mouth open and my breath harsh in my ears despite the way the breeze carried some of it away.

"Pump them into me and stroke...stroke me on the inside." She rose to meet every thrust as I worked my fingers in and out of her, curling them up to run the pads of my fingers against her throbbing inner walls.

"More. Move more." Even as gasps, I could do nothing but follow her instructions, my fingers, my arm, my body just an extension of her will, her want. I twisted and curved my fingers, filling her up as best I could and massaging every place in her I could find, until my knuckles brushed something inside that made her shout. "God yes! That!"

I moaned then, meeting the enthusiasm of her hips with fingers that truly fucked her the way that she wanted, knuckles rubbing that remarkable place that forced hot muscles to clench and shudder around me. At first, I didn't even understand her next words, half-buried among the linked-together groans.

"More... More fingers. Yes, three, four, god whatever. Just... *oh god!*" The hitched cry she gave when I worked in a third and plunged as deep as I could again and again made the ache between my own legs spread hot vibrations into my abdomen. "Don't stop!"

On my knees, looking up at her with head thrown back and strong legs spread, my fingers moving hard and fast inside her until words blurred into notes nature herself would envy, I thought: If god made such a creature as this, who could shatter the mind with beauty like this, how could this be a path to hell and not to heaven? I swore the sun haloed her head with light as she arched up from the bench, her body gripping my fingers so hard they cramped and shook, but I had never cared less about my own pain.

Words skated out with my breath before I even knew what they would be. "Thank you, miss. Thank you." I found that those were all the words I knew right then and the only way I knew to respond to the amazing gift she'd shared with me, the phrase's repetition returning again and again, if softer, as she settled back onto the bench and finally relaxed.

"Put your head on my knee," she sighed, her exhale heavy with exhaustion even as her mouth formed a small smile.

When I pressed my forehead just there against her knee, it felt like prayer at the holiest altar I'd ever knelt before, and even though my hand was still slick and aching, resting between her thighs, when she ran her fingers through my hair, I felt blessed. "Thank you," I said, more steadily this time.

"You're welcome. And you can move your arms now."

I laughed against the taut skin of her shin and gently kissed her there as I brought my wayward arms back to settle in my lap.

"Are you mine now?" I had never heard her sound so tentative, but there was a waver in her voice that made me want to see her face. She held my head against her leg, though, and wouldn't let me up.

I answered from my heart because I knew no other way to reply. "I always was, miss. I just...thought you might outgrow me."

"Goodness no." She laughed and relaxed her hold, my eyes meeting hers in afternoon light that seemed almost too bright to be real. "In fact, I think I've grown into you."

"Oh?" I blinked, not sure how that could be possible since I was fairly certain I wasn't the sort of accessory to be a size too big for someone as well put together as her.

She just smiled and traced the curve of my cheek with her fingers before pressing the tips of two over my lips. Her eyes sparkled with secrets I hoped that she'd share. "Tomorrow. I'll teach you more tomorrow."

I thought that I'd already grown up in that garden and maybe I had, but that summer I knew I'd flourish, mature and truly find my place, in her words, her hands and her will.

ABOUT THE AUTHORS

JOVE BELLE (jovebelle.com) lives in the Pacific Northwest with her wife and children. She is the author of seven novels (*The Job, Uncommon Romance, Love and Devotion, Indelible, Chaps, Split the Aces* and *Edge of Darkness*), all available from Bold Strokes Books.

J. CALADINE lives, writes and has interesting adventures in California's Bay Area. She hopes her story turns you on, and that you do something about it.

JEN CROSS's (writingourselveswhole.org) writing appears in a plethora of publications, including *Women in Lust, Nobody Passes, Gotta Have It* and many more. She's toured nationally with the Body Heat Femme Porn Tour, and facilitates erotic and trauma survivors writing workshops in Oakland and around the country.

TAMSIN FLOWERS writes lighthearted erotica, often with a twist in the tail and a sense of fun. Her stories have appeared in numerous anthologies and usually, she's working on at least ten stories at once. While she figures out whose leg belongs in which story, you can find out more at Tamsin's Superotica.

GIGI FROST (facebook.com/gigifrost), Boston-based artist and activist, serves up smut with a side of politics. She appears nationally with the Body Heat Femme Porn Tour and the Femme Show, produces queer shows, teaches, and spends her nights on any stage that will have her. Publications include stories in *Second Person Queer, Say Please* and *Girl Crazy.*

DENA HANKINS (denahankins.net) writes aboard her boat, wherever she has sailed it. After eight years as a sex educator, she started telling tales with far-flung settings—India, North Carolina and deep space—and continued with a queer/trans romance novel, *Blue Water Dreams*, about magnetism and self-sufficiency.

AIMEE HERMAN is a Brooklyn writer looking to disembowel the architecture of gender, bodies and what it means to be queer. Find Aimee's poems in *Troubling the Line: Trans and Genderqueer Poetry and Poetics* (Nightboat Books), in the full-length collection, *to go without blinking* (BlazeVOX books) and at aimeeherman.wordpress.com.

VICTORIA JANSSEN (victoriajanssen.com) has written three novels for Harlequin, including *The Duchess, Her Maid, The Groom and Their Lover*, as well as short stories. Her recent work may be found in *Morning, Noon and Night; The Mammoth Book of Best New Erotica 12* and *Sudden Sex.*

KYLE JONES writes dirty stories that will swagger and wink their way into your waking dreams, stories featuring characters with diverse genders and identities. For more from Kyle, including thoughts and writing on identity, gender, privilege, kink, poly-amory and parenting, point your browser to butchtastic.net.

AXA LEE is an erotica-writing Michigan farm girl, who grazes cattle in her yard and herds incorrigible poultry with a cowardly dog. She's written since her grandmother had to spell the words for her. Other work appears in *Shameless Behavior* and *Dirty Little Numbers*, published by Go Deeper Press.

ANNABETH LEONG's (annabethleong.blogspot.com) lesbian erotica includes *One Flesh* (Storm Moon Press), *Heated Leather Lover* (Ellora's Cave), and short stories in *Best Bondage Erotica 2014* (Cleis), *Women with Handcuffs* (Cleis), *She Who Must Be Obeyed* (Lethe Press) and many more anthologies. Follow her on Twitter @annabethleong.

SOMMER MARSDEN (sommermarsden.blogspot.com): pro-fessional dirty-word writer, gluten-free baker, sock addict, fat wiener-dog walker, expert procrastinator. Called "one of the top storytellers in the erotic genre" by Violet Blue, and author of numerous erotic novels including *Restricted Release, Boys Next Door, Restless Spirit* and *Lost in You.*

MELISSA MAYHEW loves writing romantic and erotic fiction. Her short stories include *Bend Over, Baby 1 & 2* and she has contributed to anthologies including *The Mammoth Book of Urban Erotic Confessions*. As Goldie Ledbury, she has published a novella, *Lone Star Family Values*. Melissa lives in Durham, England.

San Francisco–based writer, teacher and somatic sex coach **PAVINI MORAY** helps queer, gender-fabulous and fat clients claim their desire and live their full erotic potential. When not blogging about sex and intimacy at emancipatingsexuality.com, Pavini can be found putting on glitter and dreaming up pleasure revolutions.

D. ORCHID is a geeky mocha butch with a love of poetry, power dynamics, and stories that take readers to unexpected places alongside characters from every shade of every rainbow. Writing for wanderers at heart, D. explores joy and struggle, freedom and surrender, the sweetness and the darkness of life.

SINCLAIR SEXSMITH (mrsexsmith.com) is an erotic coach and educator. They write the award-winning online *Sugarbutch Chronicles: The Sex, Gender, and Relationship Adventures of a Kinky Queer Butch Top* (sugarbutch.net), have contributed to more than twenty anthologies and edited *Say Please: Lesbian BDSM Erotica*. They frequently teach gender and sexuality workshops.

KATHLEEN TUDOR hides out in the wilds of California with her spouse and their favorite monkey. Her wicked words have broken down the doors to presses like Cleis, Mischief Harper-Collins, Xcite and more. If you see her, please contact polykathleen@gmail.com. Keep an eye on kathleentudor.com for updates on her antics.

VICTORIA VILLASENOR is an editor for a lesbian publishing house and occasional writer, with stories in *Blood and Lipstick, She-Shifters, Women Who Bite, Women of the Dark Streets, Where the Girls Are, Women in Uniform* and *Blue Collar Lesbian Erotica*. She lives in the Midlands of England with her partner.

ANNA WATSON is a married, old-school femme who queers suburbia west of Boston and who has been writing about butch/femme sexuality for over twenty years. This story is for neighborhood characters and funny little women everywhere. You are gorgeous, sexy, fabulous. Show me. I want to see.

ABOUT
THE EDITOR

SACCHI GREEN is a Lambda Award–winning writer and editor of erotica and other stimulating genres. Her stories have appeared in scores of publications, including eight volumes of *Best Lesbian Erotica,* four of *Best Women's Erotica,* and four of *Best Lesbian Romance.* In recent years she's taken to wielding the editorial whip, editing nine lesbian erotica anthologies, most recently *Lesbian Cowboys, Girl Crazy, Lesbian Lust, Women with Handcuffs, Girl Fever* and *Wild Girls, Wild Nights,* all from Cleis Press. Sacchi lives in western Massachusetts, retreats often to the mountains of New Hampshire and can be found online at sacchi-green.blogspot.com and on Facebook.